Shooting at Loons

a Deborah Knott mystery

Margaret Maron

Shooting at Loons

Oconee Spirit Press, Waverly, TN www.oconeespirit.com

ISBN 978-0-9974575-4-4

First Oconee Spirit paperback printing: April 2017

Library of Congress Cataloging-in-Publication Data

Maron, Margaret.

Shooting at Loons/ Margaret Maron

Reprint. Originally published: Shooting at loons. New York: Mysterious Press, 1994.

1. Knott, Deborah (Fictitious character)-Fiction. 2. Women judges-Fiction. 3. North Carolina-Fiction.

10 9 8 7 6 5 4 3 2 1

Printed and bound in the United States. The text paper is SFI certified. The Sustainable Forestry Initiative® program promotes sustainable forest management.

Cover design by Paper Moon Graphics.

To Andrée

Between the tides through surf-crushed shells,
Wet from the spray of ocean swells,
You bend for a blue crab's carapace,
I for a conch pitted into lace
While the waves curl in slow parallels.
Eyes on the sand, we might each be alone.
Like a hermit crab I am ingrown
And yet, after all, very glad of your presence
To share a mussel's iridescence
Or a necklace of sun-bleached bone.
You do not deride the choices I make
Nor question the value of things I take:
Moon snails, pebbles, odd bits of dark wood—
I couldn't defend them if you should,
Though they almost ease the ache.
Between the tides for a time we walk;
And though it is of shells we talk,
We are whorled in separate shells
And dead men's fingers thumb the swells.

Harkers Island, 1975

Acknowledgments

As always, I am indebted to many for their help and should like to give special thanks to Karen Piner Campbell; Dr. Barbara Garrity-Blake, ECU Institute for Coastal and Marine Resources; Joel G. Hancock, author of *Strengthened by the Storm;* Captain Ken Craft, NC Wildlife Resources Commission; Sue and Carl Honeycutt; Donald Kirkman and Dianne Mizzell, Carteret County Economic Development Council; Darlene Leonard, Clerk of Court for Carteret County; Carol Lohr, Director, Carteret County Tourism Development Bureau; Tony Seamon, President, Carolina-in-Touch; Jerry Schill, Executive Director, NC Fisheries Association; Judith Moore Spitsbergen, author of *Seacoast Life;* Michael W. Street, NC Division of Marine Fisheries; Sheriff Ralph Thomas Jr.; Judge Jerry F. Waddell, 3B District Court District; Jule Wheatley, President, Beaufort Fisheries.

Disclaimer

While North Carolina is—happily—much more than a state of mind, it has no county named for Sir John Colleton, one of King Charles II's lords proprietors. In rectifying that omission, I should like to make it clear that my Colleton County does not portray a real place, and any resemblance between its fictional inhabitants and actual persons is purely coincidental.

Beaufort and Harkers Island are, however, real places on the southern coast of North Carolina and they are inhabited by real people, some of whom appear here by permission in cameo. Otherwise, this book is a complete work of fiction; and to fit the needs of fiction, I have peopled it with characters who do not exist outside my imagination. I have also taken liberties with the landscape: pushing some houses apart in order to set down empty lots or different houses, placing my "Ritchie House" a little further down the boardwalk from a very real (and very charming) Beaufort House, erecting a second menhaden plant where once there were several, but now only one.

CHAPTER 1

The flashlight was square, waterproof, and a bright fluorescent orange. Square, so it could sit firmly on the seat of a flounder boat, waterproof so it would float if it went over the side, Day-Glo orange so it could be easily spotted and fished out of the shallows when (not if) it did go overboard with a gill net or crab pot.

I set it atop the water tank in the small windowless pump house and held Carl's handwritten instructions up to its strong beam.

Turn off drain-out at bottom of water tank.

Check.

Close petcock bottom left of pump.

Check.

Close valve between pump and tank.

Check.

Prime with water in jugs near tank (about 1 gal.) When primed, close gate valve and plug in pump. Should click on and off a few times.

The only jugs I could see in the shadowy recess beside the pump were some yellow ones with antifreeze labels. I had to move three wire crab baskets to get at them and—

"Need some help with that?" asked a voice from the doorway behind me.

I jumped, banged my head on a pipe that ran from the ancient pump to a fairly new water tank, and turned to see an adolescent male shape in black rubber boots.

It'd been two years since I last stepped foot on Harkers Island and he'd shot up four or five inches, but there was no mistaking that sun-bleached straw thatch. Nor the ubiquitous rubber boots he wore whenever he wasn't barefooted or heading off to school in sneakers.

"Thanks, Guthrie," I said, "but I believe I can figure it out myself."

The boy elbowed aside Carl's charcoal grill and pushed in beside me. "I help Carl all the time."

The most distinctive feature of "Down East" speech is that every long *i* sound is replaced by an *oi*. In the accent of Guthrie's seafaring ancestors, the words came out *"Oi he'p Carl ahl th' toime."*

Some say that "hoi toider" (high tider) speech is a survival of pure Elizabethan; others say it's a natural product of two hundred years' isolation here near the southern end of the Outer Banks. Until a causeway and bridge were built in the forties, boats were all that connected Harkers Island to the mainland.

One of Guthrie's great-grandmothers died in a hospital over in Morehead in the mid-seventies, and that dash across North River, through Beaufort, across the Newport River channel, was the first time she'd ever been off-island in her entire eighty-some years, never mind upstate. (Her children always swore it was the shock of leaving the island that killed her, not the stroke.)

The smell of salt air and fried fish clung to Guthrie's white tee shirt as he hoisted a yellow jug from my hand.

"This what you're using to prime her with?" he asked.

"If it's clean water." I stepped back so he could get at the pump. Hey, I'm not proud. Any male, young or old, who wants to do my dirty work, he's more than welcome.

Water gurgled from the jug till it ran out through the open pump valve.

I still had my cousin's instructions in my hand. "Did you close the gate valve?"

"Yep."

I fished out the plug end of the pump cord, he pushed it into the socket, and the pump came on with a roar.

Guthrie started to back out.

"Wait! We're not done." I almost had to shout to be heard above the noisy pump as I read aloud from the crumpled sheet: *"Open valve between pump and tank little by little and open valve going into hot water tank. Pressure should build to 40 lbs. on gauge and shut off."*

"Which'un's the hot water valve?" the boy shouted back.

"I thought you said you help Carl all the time."

"Do, but he changed 'em around last time." He suddenly twisted a cutoff knob on one of the many pipes. "That's her," he declared.

The pump continued to labor and the pressure gauge wouldn't go beyond 15. I pointed this out to Guthrie.

"Give 'er some more time," he said and leaned back, prepared to make small talk above the noise. "Carl coming down?"

"No." I eyed the pressure gauge. "Just me this trip."

"When you going back?"

"Thursday or Friday maybe." Today was Sunday in early April. "We're still not getting any pressure."

"Reckon you didn't turn off all the spigots?" he asked, ready to disclaim any part of a malfunction.

"Everything I saw. Except for one on the outside shower so the air'll bleed out."

"I'll go see if she's putting out water," he volunteered.

Now that he was gone and it was just me and the pump, I realized I could hear water spilling from somewhere. In fact, I could feel water oozing into my sneakers. I seemed to be standing in a puddle. Shining the flashlight at the bottom of the water tank, I saw yet another open tap through which water was gushing. Once I closed it, the gauge needle finally crept up to 40 psi and the pump shut off.

Into the silence came the cry of gulls and a lapping of gentle swells.

"She worn't spitting air anymore and I closed her off," Guthrie reported. He eyed the gauge complacently. "Reckon that's all she needed."

"'Preciate your help," I told him as we both stepped out into bright sunlight.

⌘

Harkers Island lies across from the Cape Lookout Lighthouse on an east-west axis, and I always have trouble getting oriented down here. When you look out over the sound to Shackleford Banks, you feel that because it's seawater and Shackleford's part of the Outer Banks, you must be looking east. In reality, you're looking almost due south.

The wind was coming from the west, blowing off the land, and it was warm and springlike. Beyond a grassy hump too low to be called a dune, the water of Back Sound lay smooth as one of my daddy's freshwater fish ponds.

Behind us, nestled amongst three live oaks and some overgrown privet, was the small shabby clapboard cottage that had been built around 1910. Like most older houses down here, the builder had been a waterman, not a professional carpenter: the high-pitched roof originally covered four tiny rooms and shedded off over a front porch, with a hand pump and privy somewhere out behind. Even though Carl and Sue had added a bath and new kitchen across the back, brought in electricity and running water, reshingled the roof, and painted the warped clapboards a cheerful yellow, if you held your head just right, you could see daylight through some cracks and it still looked as if the first big wind ought to blow it slam across the island. Yet there it sat, despite eighty years of hurricanes and nor'easters.

Behind the cottage was a thicket of yaupon bushes and, beyond those, Clarence Willis's mobile home faced the road and helped buffer the cottage from weekend traffic to the Shell Point ferry in the summer. The Willises, father and son, were watermen and boat builders like Guthrie's grandfather; but they were to be away all week, according to Carl.

Carl and Sue are my distant cousins. At least, Sue is. On my mother's Stephenson side. Their daughters are my age and I used to come down with them several times a year all through childhood and adolescence.

Between my brothers and their wives and a bunch of aunts and uncles, I can't turn around in Colleton County without somebody telling someone else; so when Carl heard through the family grapevine that I'd been assigned to fill in at the Carteret County courthouse for an ailing judge, he insisted that I stay at their place. "We haven't been down since February," he said, "so all the water's still cut off, but that's no problem."

Well, no, not if you don't mind groping around up under the edge of the house for a half-dozen cutoff valves before you even tackle the pump itself. The house sits on low brick pilings, no skirting, no foundation, open to every blast of winter storms. Every time an exposed pipe freezes and bursts, Carl installs a new spigot so the pipe can be drained at that point, never mind the obstacles.

Guthrie was sucking at a bleeding knuckle where he'd knocked the scab off.

"Floor joist got me," he said sheepishly.

I saw the other scabbed knuckles on his fist, then noticed a half-healed cut on his round chin. And although it had faded to a pale blue shadow, I could make out the remains of a bruise on the cheekbone beneath his right eye.

"Must have been quite a fight," I observed.

"Ah, naw. Fell in my boat," he said, sounding enough like one of my nephews to make it clear he didn't plan to talk about it.

Fine with me. As a district court judge, I have to listen to too many stories of who took the first swing after who said what to go looking for yet another.

"When'd you get a boat?" I asked.

"November, when I turned fourteen," said Guthrie.

"Your granddaddy give it to you?" I smiled, thinking how island kids must look forward to a first boat the way I'd looked forward to my first car.

"Naw, I worked out the money fishing and clamming."

I forget what it was that killed his mother when he was two or three. Ruptured appendix? Or was it pneumonia? I'm pretty sure it was something that didn't have to be fatal if she'd gotten treatment in time; but her husband was off pulling a drunk or something, and she just lay there in that trailer parked on the backside of nowhere and died.

Mickey Mantle Davis was too wild and shiftless to make a home for any child, so he dumped Guthrie on his parents and, as far as I could see, if he contributed anything to the boy's upbringing, it was more as an older brother might than as a real father should.

As the boy and I talked, we'd been walking past wind-sculpted live oaks, across the flat grassy stretch that lay between the cottage and a knee-high ridge of sand that rose from the water's edge. A short path had been worn through the mini-dune and we stepped through it onto the beach. Not that there's much of a beach here. Even at dead low tide, there's only a few feet of clear sand and that's usually littered with kelp, an occasional boot or stray sneaker, conch shells, plastic six-pack rings or torn fishing nets. Being on the sound side of Shackleford Banks, waves here are generally just wavelets, lazy and gentle with hardly any break at all unless there's a storm kicking up.

East of us was a wildish stretch that fronted an empty field. To the west was Mahlon Davis's narrow landing, then another field, this one overgrown with yucca, wax myrtle and sumac. Along Mahlon's line, and spilling over in places on that side, were an abandoned truck, a hodge-podge of raised cockerel pens and enough trash and debris to fill several dumpsters. At least the Davises had quit piling it along Carl's line.

Sand fleas skittered away from our feet, and the terns and sandpipers that had flown up as we approached now resumed their inspection of the water's edge a safe distance away.

Early afternoon and the tide was still low, but coming in. There was a funky smell of wet seaweed, salt water, and clumps of drying eel grass. Otherwise, the air was so crystalline that the black-and-white diamond-patterned lighthouse stood out crisply, and the sun was so dazzling that it almost cancelled the distant light that gleamed and flashed every fifteen seconds. Out in the channel, speedboats zoomed past, trailing wakes that rocked some pelicans that were floating with a few sea gulls a hundred feet offshore. Where the shoreline curved, more gulls lifted from the carcass of a rusted-out car and flew over to see if we happened to have stale bread or were dumping any fish offal. They voiced their disappointment in raucous cries when no food appeared and settled onto several small boats that were moored in close.

For several long minutes I just breathed it all in, feeling what Julia Lee's poodle must feel when it slips the leash and heads for the woods. A whole week ahead of me. Five full days in a place where no one who knew me would have the right to make cracks about the way I dressed or drove or drank.

Like Julia Lee's CoCo, I don't get too many chances to run wild these days. Not that I planned to emulate CoCo, who's never been spayed—despite what my brothers think, I *have* learned a little judicious discretion. Still, if I did take a notion to run through the underbrush, it was nice to know that my nearest nosey brother was more than a hundred miles away.

"That your boat?" I asked Guthrie, pointing to a white skiff with a dark red bottom.

"Naw, that's Mark's," he said, naming another neighboring teenager. "Yonder's mine." He gestured proudly.

Sporting a recent coat of fresh white paint, the skiff was flat-bottomed, with a flared bow, two board seats, and a black outboard motor.

"Your granddaddy build it?" I asked, remembering that Mahlon Davis had begun framing a skiff the last time I was down. Now a trawler was taking shape beyond the boat shelter beside their house.

Harkers Islanders are famous all up and down the Atlantic Coast as independent boat builders who use lore handed down from generation to generation. Most boat works are one- or two-man operations. A man needs a fishing boat, he doesn't have to go buy it. He can build it. Houses may get thrown together, but little skiffs aren't much challenge to men who can build anything that floats, from yachts to fishing schooners, with no plans or blueprints, just by "rack of the eye."

"He helped me," Guthrie said, "but I did most of the work."

He waded out to the boat and fiddled with the propeller blades with that proprietary air men always seem to have about boats or trucks. Teetering on the verge of manhood now. Fourteen and a half. His preadolescent chubbiness was almost gone, his belly was flattening, his muscles tightening.

But when he splashed back to shore, he was still a diffident kid. "Want to see how she rides?"

Being banged around the sound in a flat-bottomed skiff was a far cry from skimming across the surface in a streamlined power cruiser. Still . . .

"Wouldn't know where I could dig a few clams for supper, would you?" I asked.

"Other side of the channel, over near the banks is good." Boyish eagerness to show off was suddenly tinged with crafty materialism. "Wouldn't take more'n five dollars worth of gas."

As I made a show of considering, he added, "Carl's got two rakes. I'd help you dig 'em."

⌘

Ten minutes later, I'd changed into shorts, a windbreaker and a raggedy old pair of Sue's sneakers and we were heading out to the channel, a five-gallon plastic bucket and two clam rakes stowed in the bow. Despite April sunshine, the air was nippy out on the water, but I left the jacket unzipped and the hood down. Wind streamed through my hair and salt spray misted my face. Guthrie sat in the stern with his hand on the tiller and the throttle wide open. If he was chilly in just a tee shirt, he didn't show it.

A dispossessed gull followed us for a couple of minutes, then wheeled off toward Beaufort and Morehead City.

Sunday afternoon and the channel was still sprinkled with upstate boaters and recreational fishermen—"dingbatters and ditdots" in scornful island parlance. Soon most of them would be swinging in to launch ramps along the shore, pulling their boats out of the water and heading on back up to Raleigh, Asheville, Greensboro. By sunset, Highway 70 West would be bumper-to-bumper with boat trailers, RVs, and shiny pickups, all with a cooler or two of fresh fish and steamer clams.

I knew because I'd been part of that Sunday night exodus enough weekends myself. It always seemed so luxurious the few times I'd stayed over till a Monday or Tuesday.

Instead of bucking Sunday night traffic, I planned to pop a cool one, prop my feet on the porch railing and enjoy the sunset while a big pot of clam chowder simmered on the stove for my supper. Core Sound chowder can taste right thin to folks raised on the Manhattan or New England varieties, but my mouth watered as I wondered if there was any cornmeal back at the house for dumplings. Not that it mattered since I'd probably have to run up to Cab's store anyhow and buy a piece of salt pork to season the chowder with.

We cut across the wake of a hotshot cigarette and the flat bottom of the skiff smacked the waves as hard as if we were riding on dirt roads rutted like a washboard. My face tingled with the unmistakable combination of wind, salt and sun, and my hair tangled in my sunglasses as it whipped about my head, but I didn't care. Even jouncing along in a homemade, no-frills skiff, it was exhilarating to be out on a broad expanse of water again, to know that if we headed due east from the lighthouse, the next land we'd hit would be the coast of North Africa.

Not that I'm all that comfortable when I'm totally out of the sight of land. In some ways the empty inland deserts of North Africa would be no more incomprehensible to me than these coastal waters once I get too far offshore to pick out landmarks. Desert nomads, Arctic Eskimos and Core Sounders have been firmly linked in my mind ever since I heard that nomads can read dust clouds and Eskimos can differentiate between more than forty separate types of snow.

More than once when I was a girl, my cousins and their little brother and I would be lolling out in the warm shallows, the air hot and still, the sky above as cloudless as an empty blue bowl, too enervated by the still air to do more than keep our sunburned skin under water and out of the reach of stinging dogflies.

Suddenly we'd see a half-dozen men come striding down to their boats with quick urgency, splashing past us in boots and waders to hoist themselves up over the sides.

"What's happening?" we'd call.

"She's a-turning," Mahlon Davis would grunt as he lifted anchor and lowered his motor to head out to his favorite set. "Don't you feel her turning?"

We'd look at each other blankly while the little boats roared out to the channel, leaving us tossed in their wake. A few minutes later, we would feel a tentative stirring, nothing more than a promise of breeze. Then would come that gradual but steady push as the wind freshened and turned and blew straight in off the water.

"How did they know?" we asked ourselves in wonder.

⌘

As we left the channel and angled over into the shallows, Guthrie throttled back on the Evinrude and the boat lay flatter in the water till I could feel the gentle surge of slow waves. Within minutes, we were coasting across undulating grasses only inches below the surface as we drifted in toward Shackleford. I sighted a familiar-looking sandbar that I seemed to remember from an earlier trip although I didn't recall those stakes sticking up above high-water level.

⌘

"What's that?" I called back to Guthrie.

"Leased bottom."

"Huh? You can rent the sea bottom?"

"Got enough money, you can do anything you dang well feel like."

We circled closer and I saw now that the stakes defined about three acres of the sandbar and were posted with signs from one of the state's governmental divisions stating that this was a shellfish bottom leased by a Heston Hadley for the cultivation of clams. I seemed to remember now some mention of this new practice in the *News and Observer,* but it hadn't affected me, so I hadn't paid much attention.

Guthrie had. "Danged old Marine Fisheries," he huffed. "You can rent you a square mile off 'em if you got the money. Then you can keep everybody else off even if they've been clamming or oystering in that spot their whole lives."

He spat overboard in disgust. "Gonna be so proggers can't take a fish or clam anywhere in the sound. Whole dang place'll be leased out."

Clearly, Guthrie didn't approve of leased bottoms. Didn't sound fair to me either, for that matter.

Several hundred feet away, at the far side of the stakes, we saw another skiff bobbing at its anchor line. Its motor had been raised to keep the propeller from dragging on the bottom.

To my eye, it could have been the twin of the skiff we were in, but Guthrie took one look and said, "Andy Bynum's."

I brightened. Andy Bynum was a semi-retired fisherman who lived across the road from the cottage and often walked through Carl's yard to get to his boats when any were moored out front. In fact, Carl had bought the cottage with the deeded stipulation that Bynums yet unborn would have access to the water in perpetuity.

Out of courtesy, when Carl and Sue were down, he often dropped off a bucket of crabs or a bushel of oysters—whatever was in season; and he would perch on the edge of their porch if offered a beer and tell wonderful stories about life on and around the water. My cousins and I never knew if he was stretching the truth or not, but we'd be laughing so hard it wouldn't matter.

I was grinning now, hoping he'd come back for his skiff before Guthrie and I finished clamming, wondering if I could tempt him to sit a spell on his way past the cottage. He was of that older generation that sometimes thinks it's improper to visit with an unchaperoned woman. Then I glanced at Guthrie's face and my grin faded at his scowl.

"What's Andy up to out here?" he asked. "Andy wouldn't take clams off'n Hes Hadley's lease."

Was he implying that we would?

Not that the whole sandbar was staked off. There was still an un-marked wedge of grassy bottom beyond the stakes, over where Bynum's skiff was rocking in the gentle surges.

Water barely covered the propeller blades as Guthrie poled us over to the empty skiff. Something about the set of his body and wary eyes made me start to tense up even though I didn't see any cause. On the other hand, I don't always understand island etiquette. Was clamming around the edges of a man's leased bottom anything like poaching crabs from someone else's pots or tearing through someone's set nets? In the years I'd been coming down to this seemingly peaceful area, I'd seen short tempers flare over the dumbest things. Some had even ended in fist fights, warning shots and outright feuds that persisted for two or three generations.

We rounded the skiff and Guthrie cut his motor. Into the sudden silence came the ever-present sound of lapping water and something else. A hollow bumping noise.

A white plastic five-gallon bucket lay on its side between a water-soaked log and the deserted skiff, and it bumped against the wooden stern with every surging swell of incoming tide.

Then we drew closer and I realized that the half-submerged log was a human figure lying face down in the shallow water.

Guthrie threw out his anchor and was over the side a half step ahead of me. "Andy must've fell on his rake," he said as we nearly tripped on the long-handled tool ourselves. Together we rolled him over and off the prongs. A half-dozen small crabs fell from his bloodied shirt to scuttle back into the chilly water. A gush of pink flowered in the sand where gouts of blood had been trapped by the weight of his body. Any idea I had of resuscitation disappeared as soon as I saw sand and grass in his open, unblinking eyes. I felt the stiffness of rigor in his arms and legs, saw the ashy paleness of his skin, and knew that the salty water had helped to leach away most of his life's blood.

"We can put him in his skiff and tow it back to shore," said Guthrie.

"No," I said. All that blood on Andy Bynum's waterlogged cotton shirt had not been caused by the blunt prongs of any clam rake. "We better not disturb things any further. You go call the police. Tell them Andy Bynum's been shot."

He didn't blink an eye. Fish aren't the only creatures brought home bloody on the boats; and at fourteen-going-on-fifteen, he's probably seen his share of violent death.

"Tide's coming in," was all he said. "Reckon you can hold him here?"

"If I have to," I answered.

I've seen my share of violent deaths, too.

CHAPTER 2

For several minutes after Guthrie roared back toward Harkers Island, I continued to stand indecisively on the edge of the sandbar until my feet were nearly numb from the chilly water washing over them.

I'd heard so many horror stories about goof-ups messing over a crime scene that I really hated to touch Andy Bynum's skiff. Reason said he'd probably been shot from another boat while he was standing on the sandbar digging for clams. Reason said that even if the killer had waded right up to the body, the incoming tide now covered every footprint. But reason could say till my feet fell off and I'd still feel skittish about getting into that skiff.

A creosoted piling stuck up like a sawed-off telephone pole near the corner of Heston Hadley's boundary. Barnacles and mussels had cemented themselves all the way up to high-water mark. Once upon a time the piling'd probably had a flat top; now it had been gouged by storms and surging tides. Nevertheless, I scrambled up to sit with my legs dangling. My bottom protested as I eased myself down. It felt like sitting on a handful of uneven pencil nubs. The water was only a few inches below my wet sneakers and beginning to wash higher with each passing moment.

A variety of sea birds swooped past—every time I come down to the coast, I swear that I'm going to bring along a book next time and learn the names of the different gulls and terns. Channel traffic had dwindled off, and although it dried my shorts and still warmed my legs and thighs, the sun was starting its long slide down the sky.

A perfect lazy April Sunday on the water.

Except for Andy Bynum's body.

The wavelets that lapped my piling, that were lifting the beached skiff from the sandbar, that emptied the bucket's clams and oysters and banged it against the skiff with steady rhythm—those same wavelets were breaking against Andy's body and I couldn't not look.

When we'd first turned him over on his back, his face was out of the water. Now his white hair fanned out around his head like mermaid's hair algae and only his mouth and chin were still clear. If help didn't come soon, he'd be totally awash and the prospect horrified me. I've always had a fear of drowning. In my worst nightmares, I'm sinking down, down through fathoms of dark water, my lungs bursting with the need for air; and even though I knew Andy Bynum would never breathe again, it was all I could do not to go kneel beside him and lift his white head clear.

Except for those open blue eyes, his face was peaceful and serene, a face as weathered as this piling I was perched on. I hoped death had been instantaneous for him. That he'd been dead before he inhaled a single drop.

A good man. Someone liked and respected by his neighbors.

("So far as you know," reminded the cautious preacher who lurks at the edges of my mind. *"There is not a just man upon earth, that doeth good and sinneth not.")*

("True," nodded the pragmatist that keeps him company.)

Okay. So what did I actually know of Andy Bynum?

Not much, now that I considered.

Probably in his early sixties. His wife had died eight or ten years ago and he'd lived alone since then in a sturdy, unpretentious brick house across the road from Carl and Sue's cottage. Two sons who were both older than me. I'd never heard of any friction between father and sons; and the last time Carl had mentioned Andy to me, he said Andy'd turned his two big boats over to the sons and was cutting back on his hours at the fish house his own father had started back in the thirties.

What else?

Well, he'd liked an occasional beer. Had never said no when Carl offered him one. "Just don't disfurnish yourself," he'd say, making sure Carl wasn't handing over the last one in his cooler.

And he liked to make people laugh with tales of his younger, roguish days. Even though it'd been years since he'd aimed a gun at a loon or turtle, Andy had once hunted both endangered species with enthusiasm.

"But I shot my last loon twenty years ago," he told us. "There'd been a piece in the paper about how they was dying out and I'd been feeling right bad about it even though we all knew them Canadians was the ones really hurting the loon population. They used the eggs for glue or something. Didn't even give the babies time to hatch out. Anyhow, it was March and me and some fellows was over on Shackleford freezing our own tailfeathers off and I had this fancy new Winchester I give a man in Portsmouth three hundred dollars for. Raiford and me, we was 'way down the dune ready to fire when we heard two gunshots, then nothing. It'd commenced to rain a little and Raiford walked up on the sandbank and looked over to see what was happening, and there was the game warden writing everybody out a ticket. Raiford sort of slithered back down the sandbank and commenced scooping us out a hole and we buried both guns 'fore you could say 'magistrate's court' three times.

"Then we got back in my skiff and was sitting there all innocent like when the game warden come around that hummock of grass. 'Y'all part of this loon hunt?' he yells out to us. 'Loon hunt?' says Raiford. 'Ain't that against the law?'

"'Bout then, that drizzle started getting serious and game wardens always did make Raiford nervous, so he started the motor and we come on back to the island and waited till it slacked off and the game warden was gone. And don't you know we couldn't remember exactly where we'd buried them two guns. Took us three days 'fore we scratched 'em out again."

Like many a reformed rogue, Andy had become a staunch upholder of the law, even game laws. Nevertheless, the last time I was down, he ruefully admitted it was still hard for him to refuse an invitation to pull up a chair when the table held a dish of stewed loon.

As water ballooned his shirt, I saw a moon snail emerge from beneath the collar. It must have been trapped when we turned the body. As soon as it pulled itself free, it dropped down into the green undulating grasses that intertwined with his hair. Small dark shapes scuttled across Andy's chest.

The crabs were back.

Without a watch, there was no way to know how long Guthrie had been gone. Ten minutes? Twenty?

As my eyes strained for shore, they were suddenly caught by a speed-boat that was heading straight out toward me from a point further down the island. One person, a slender figure in a blue shirt, stood at the wheel and held a fast course that implied intimate familiarity with this particular stretch of the sound. Guthrie had already cut his engine by the time he was this far beyond the channel, but this boater was either suicidal or else knew to the precise second how long to keep the propeller down.

The motor cut off just as I was expecting to see churned sand and fouled blades, and the continued impetus carried the boat across the shallows to end up less than thirty feet away.

It was a woman about my age, mid-thirties, in white shorts, short blonde hair and those mirrored sunglasses that I hate because you never get a reading on the person's eyes. I particularly hate them when the wearer's carrying a .22 rifle like this unsmiling woman was. She held it loosely, with a casual ease that implied the same expertise as she'd already shown with her boat handling.

"Mind telling me what you're doing out here?"

"Waiting for the police," I answered, in case she decided to start pointing that thing. I gestured toward Andy Bynum's body, but his skiff blocked her view and she didn't immediately grasp the situation.

Although the volume was turned way down, I could hear the staticky chatter of a CB radio from the dashboard as she propped the rifle on the seat of her boat, swung over the edge into thigh-deep water that would have had me flinching and moaning, and pulled her boat over to tie up at a marker stake near me.

"What's the law got to do with Andy's—" That's when she saw him. "Good Lord Jesus! What happened?"

She waded nearer. Tiny minnows darted in and out of the dead man's white hair and an ooze of red continued to flower from his chest.

"Looks like someone shot him," I said.

"So that's why Mahlon Davis took off so fast and left you out here by yourself."

"That was Guthrie, not his grandfather." I eased down from the piling and faced her. "Mind telling me how come you were watching us so closely?"

She gestured toward the line of stakes that enclosed most of the sandbank. "My husband Hes and me, this is our leased bottom."

Before I could ask why that required an armed investigation, she splashed back to her boat, pulled herself in and reached for her CB mike. "Hadley to base. Over."

Through the static, I heard a female voice. "What's happening, Mom? Over."

"Call Marvin Willitt. See if he's heard he's needed out here. Out."

She replaced the mike and those mirrored glasses reflected my image. Well, two could play that game. My sunglasses were perched up in my hair and I pulled them down over my eyes like a mask as I asked, "Who's Marvin Willitt?"

"Sheriff's deputy for down east. Assigned to Harkers Island. You staying on the island?"

"Yes."

"You knew Andy?"

"Yes, I knew him." My feet were starting to go numb again. "Look, you mind if I sit in your boat?"

"Help yourself."

Not the most gracious invitation I'd ever had.

She watched my ineffectual effort to hoist myself gracefully over the side, then grudgingly said, "Give me your hand."

I was hauled up onto cracked vinyl seats of sun-faded blue with lumpy foam. After that rough-topped piling though, they felt like goosedown cushions.

"I'm Jay Hadley," said the woman, suddenly pushing her glasses up into sun-streaked blonde hair. Sea-green eyes squinted in the sudden brightness and I saw that they were pooled with tears.

"Deborah Knott," I said.

The radio crackled into speech.

"Willitt to Hadley. Jay? You out there, over?"

Her voice didn't quaver.

"Yeah, Marvin. Over."

"Guthrie Davis says there's been a accident out by your bottom lease. He telling the truth, over?"

"Yeah, this time. Over."

"Sit tight then. We'll be right out. Out."

A minute later, the same young woman's voice spoke through the static. "Base to Hadley. Mom? Who's hurt? Over."

"Tell you later, Becca. Over and out." She hung up the mike with finality.

"Your daughter?"

Again the brusque nod. "Where you staying on the island?"

"That yellow cottage across from Andy's place, catty-corner from Mahlon Davis's."

She studied me openly. "I thought their names was Carlette and Celeste."

"My cousins. You know them?"

"Not to know," she said shortly.

I suddenly realized that this was about the longest one-on-one conversation I'd ever had with an island woman. The men might wander over when Carl was on the porch or out in the yard working on his lawn mower or fiddling with some maintenance chores, but seldom the women. If we happened to be hanging our bathing suits out on the line to dry or if we walked into the store when a wife or daughter we knew by sight was also there, they'd nod or speak, but never more than what was absolutely necessary for politeness. Sue had somehow endeared herself to Miss Nellie Em, Mahlon's mother (and Guthrie's great-grandmother), and the old woman will even come inside for a glass of tea; but she never visits unless Sue is there.

As for the other neighbor women, whether from pride or clannishness, they keep themselves to themselves so far as most upstaters are concerned; and Mahlon's wife Effrida is almost a pure-out recluse. The only time I ever see her outside is going to or from church or to hang out clothes.

"You knew Andy pretty well?" I asked.

"Whole island knows Andy. Whole sound, for that matter. Even up in Raleigh. He started the Alliance and he used to be on the Marine Fisheries Commission. He quit it though when it got took over too bad by pier owners and dingbatters."

I was amused. "You mean sports fishermen from upstate?"

"Sportsmen." She almost spat the word. "They'd run us right on off the water and out of the sound if they could."

Andy Bynum's face was totally awash now. Small fishes darted over his open eyes and explored his half-parted lips. Leave him here three days and there'd be nothing left but bones that would quickly pit and calcify and dissolve back into the ocean.

"Full fathom five thy father lies," quoted Jay Hadley, unexpectedly paralleling my thoughts.

"Of his bones are coral made.
Those are pearls that were his eyes
Nothing of him that doth fade,
But doth suffer a sea-change
Into something rich and strange."

Okay, I admit it: I stared at her in mouth-open astonishment.

She pulled those mirrored sunglasses back over her eyes. "We ain't all totally ignorant down here." Her voice was half-embarrassed, half-belligerent. "Or maybe you think William Shakespeare's something else that belongs to just you rich upstaters?"

"Of course not," I answered, stung by how close to the truth she was.

We rocked in the easy swells. A few miles over, the ferry was returning from Cape Lookout to Shell Point at the end of the island. She maneuvered our boat closer to Andy's body and made angry shooing motions with her hands. The little fish scattered.

I tried to look dispassionately at his sodden shirt.

19

"Hard to tell if that blood's caused by an entrance or exit wound," I mused. "I hope the bullet's still inside him, though, so they'll be able to match the weapon."

Now it was her turn to stare. "You something with the law?"

"A judge," I admitted. "I'll be holding district court in Beaufort tomorrow."

Suddenly, Jay Hadley stood and, in one practiced motion, raised the .22 and cracked off a shot into the edge of her clam bed.

"Stingray," she said blandly.

I twisted in the boat and peered between the piling and the stake over to the far edge of the leased area where the bullet had struck, but I saw nothing. "Where?"

"Guess I missed. Don't see it now."

She stowed the rifle on a pair of hooks under the dash and pointed to a sleek white cruiser heading toward us from the northwest, the direction of Beaufort and Morehead City.

"Yonder comes the rescue boat."

⌘

Since becoming an attorney, I've observed the processing of more than one crime scene; and although this was the first time I'd watched police officers do one out on an ocean with the tide coming in, I felt I could mention a few things, even though Dwight Bryant, the sheriff's deputy back in Dobbs, always acts like I'm meddling instead of helping when I suggest things to him.

"Before you move the body," I said, "hadn't you ought to take a picture of how he's lying?"

The detective in rolled-up chinos and sports shirt ignored me as he felt for a pulse we all knew was lacking, but the uniformed Marvin Willitt said, "Guthrie told me y'all turned him over soon as you found him."

"We did," I agreed. "But we didn't shift him around much, just rolled him straight over from his stomach to his back."

"You didn't try to resuscitate him?" asked the detective who'd waded over from the rescue boat. It was too big to come in all the way and was anchored out from the sandbar.

I shook my head. "His skin was cold and it felt like rigor was already beginning when we turned him," I explained.

They gave me an odd look.

"She's a judge," said Jay Hadley.

That got me another odd look and I could sense an *us versus her* line being drawn in the water; but the detective splashed back to the boat and got a Polaroid camera. While another uniformed officer helped Willitt pull a tape measure from Bynum's body to the fixed pilings, the detective measured the temperature of the water and then started sketching a rough diagram of the things he'd just photographed. He drew the position of the heavy rake, the empty bucket, the smooth clams and razor-rough oysters, the position of the anchor, and, of course, Andy's body.

By this time, Jay Hadley's boat had been shoved over beside the rescue boat, the two of us still in it, and a second detective, Quig Smith, hitched her line to one of his cleats so he could question us easily.

Guthrie had not returned, but he'd evidently given the broad outlines to Willitt when he phoned from the local quick stop. Mostly I just confirmed what Guthrie had already told them: no, I hadn't noticed Bynum's skiff till we were nearly on it; no, I hadn't seen another boat leaving that area; no, I wouldn't say that the body was rigid with rigor, merely beginning to stiffen.

Thank you, Judge, and now for Miz Hadley.

Yes, they kept a pair of glasses by the kitchen window, said Jay Hadley. "Ever since that trouble last month, we're sort of in the habit that whoever's passing'll take a quick look."

Detective Quig Smith nodded as if "that trouble last month" was old news. "You see Andy get here?"

"He was just stepping out of his skiff when we got back from church about twelve-thirty," she said. "Once I knew it was him, I didn't have to keep looking. I figured he'd be a couple of hours and things'd be fine long as he was here."

Her faint island accent turned *fine* to *foine*.

"Next time I remembered to look, there worn't a sign of Andy, just his boat. I thought maybe he hitched a ride outside with one of his boys or something. Then the *next* time, it was her and one of the Davises. I saw them get out and mess around and then he took off back to the island by hisself, and that's when I decided I'd come out and see what was going on."

"How come your husband or son didn't come out?"

"Hes had to go to Raleigh and Josh——"

A call on the police radio interrupted her and Smith had to go forward into the cabin to pick up. Whoever was calling had such a thick accent I could only catch scattered phrases and Andy Bynum's name.

"Durn!" said Jay Hadley when Smith came back down to the stern with a grimace on his face.

"What?" I asked.

"Some fool put it on the air," he said in disgust.

"It's Andy's boys," Jay Hadley told me. "They're both outside, probably halfway to the Gulf Stream, can't get back for hours. They didn't ought to have to hear about their daddy over a shortwave. Who was the blabbermouth?"

"Probably Guthrie," Smith guessed. He sighed. "Might as well let you ladies get back to shore for now."

I pointed out that I no longer had transportation.

Smith and Miz Hadley locked eyes a moment, then she nodded. "She can ride with me."

⌘

The trip back was more leisurely than I'd expected from her breakneck speed out. She leaned back in the blue vinyl seat with one hand on the wheel. The wind barely ruffled our hair. We might have been riding around Dobbs in a convertible.

More to make conversation than anything else, I asked, "When did they start renting out parcels of the sound?"

"You mean when did the great state of North Carolina realize fishermen need to earn a living off the water even though sportsmen and developers and so-called conservationists keep trying to put us out of business?" Her tone was dry, but not actively hostile at the moment.

"Is that what they're doing?"

She shrugged. "We seem to get all the rules and regulations. Turtle excluders, bycatch limits, size limits, equipment limits, right-to-sell licenses—leased bottoms are 'bout the only thing we've got back and now they're even having second thoughts about that."

"Can you just pick wherever you want? That used to be a pretty popular spot when I was a girl."

"You might've gone digging back there when you were a girl," she said, turning the wheel so that we were angling across the empty channel toward the cottage, "but that sandbar's pretty near clammed out. For me and Hes to lease it, a Marine Fisheries biologist had to certify that it's no longer a productive natural shellfish bed. That means it worn't producing ten bushels a year."

"So how do you farm it? Strew seed clams right into the sand?"

"We could. Some folks do. What me and Hes do's more costly to start with, but gets us a higher return. We load mesh bags with eight to twelve hundred seed clams and stake them on the bottom. Takes about two years to grow them out at least an inch thick."

As she warmed to her subject, the woman was downright chatty.

"Mesh bags? Like potato bags?"

"Onion bags're what we use when we harvest them. We grow them in big nylon bags about five feet square."

"Makes 'em easy to pull up," I guessed.

"Yeah, but mostly it's to protect the clams from crabs and rays and conchs. They'll wreck a regular shellfish bed." Jay Hadley gazed back over her shoulder at the staked area of water receding behind us. "We expect to harvest a thousand clams a bag next year."

I was never any good at mental math, but it didn't take an Einstein to realize that with three acres of bags staked down out there and each clam selling for nine to twenty cents apiece depending on the season, it was like leaving bags of money lying around for the taking.

"Sounds like an easy way for other people to go home with a quick bucket of clams," I mused.

"Tell me about it."

"So that's why you keep such a sharp eye on that spot." And why she came out with a gun? "Had much poaching?"

"Not bad as some folk."

If poaching was part of last month's trouble, she wasn't going to elaborate.

The yellow cottage loomed up ahead of us and the tide was now high enough that she could come in fairly close.

"Here okay?" she asked, wallowing in until the lifted propeller almost scraped bottom.

"Fine," I told her.

⌘

The sun was just sinking below the live oak trees beyond Mahlon Davis's boat shed at the water's edge and several gray-haired men were standing over there talking to him as I squished up the path to the cottage. I nodded gravely. Equally grave, they returned my nod but didn't speak or call over a question though they had to be curious about what had happened out there.

Guthrie's skiff was moored to the end of Mahlon's dilapidated dock, near where Jay Hadley dropped me off, but of Guthrie himself there was no sign. Carl's two clam rakes were propped on the edge of the porch next to the bucket.

Empty, of course.

Just as well. I certainly didn't feel like messing with clams at this point.

Instead, after changing into dry sneakers and a pair of jeans, I fixed myself a stiff bourbon and Diet Pepsi and dumped a can of Vienna sausages onto a paper plate. Saltines were in an airtight tin and I added them to the plate, then carried everything out to the porch and one of Sue's slat-bottomed rocking chairs.

I might not be eating chowder and Andy Bynum would never again perch over there with a cold beer in his hand and regale us with tall tales of island living, but nothing was going to stop me from sitting here as the Cape Lookout light got brighter and brighter in the distance, remembering how things used to be.

The men with Mahlon dispersed and all was quiet for an hour or two.

⌘

Guthrie came over at first dark. He stopped out in the yard and said, "Grandpap brought home some oysters today and Granny says do you want some since you didn't get clams?"

"Thank her for me, but I don't think so."

He started back.

"Guthrie?"

"I can't stay," he called over his shoulders. "Granny said come right back."

⌘

It was full dark, the wind was blowing straight in off the sound, and I was half sloshed when they materialized at the end of the porch, two shapes silhouetted against the security light out at the east edge of the yard.

It'd been so long since I'd seen them to know who I was looking at, that I wouldn't have recognized them.

"Evening," I said. "It's Drew and Maxton, isn't it?"

"Evening," said Andy's older son. "They say you're a judge now."

"Yes."

"They said you found him," said the younger.

"Me and Guthrie."

"Yeah, well."

"We'd rather hear it from you," said Maxton.

"If you don't mind," Drew added.

So again I told them exactly how we'd gone out to the sandbar and how we'd found their father lying in the water, stone dead. "I'm really sorry," I told them, when I'd finished. "I didn't know him very well, but what I knew, I liked. Can I get you something to drink?"

"No, thank you, ma'am."

"But we thank you for asking."

And then they were gone.

Without going on over to talk to Guthrie.

Inside the phone began to ring. I got up unsteadily and followed the trill to Sue and Carl's bedside table.

"Judge Knott?" asked a quietly cultured voice. "Judge Deborah Knott?"

"Yes?"

"Oh I am so glad I caught you! This is Linville Pope of Pope Properties? Judge Mercer is a real good friend of mine and he said for me to look after you. Could you possibly stop by on Tuesday after court for cocktails? I have asked some friends in and I know they would just love to meet you."

I looked down at my empty glass. My daddy used to lecture me about drinking alone.

"Why certainly," I said, putting on my own cultured voice. "How kind of you to ask me."

CHAPTER 3

From Greenland's icy mountains,
From India's coral strand,
Where Afric's sunny fountains
Roll down their golden sand:
From many an ancient river,
From many a palmy plain,
They call us to deliver
Their land from error's chain.

—Reginald Heber

After Bath in Beaufort County and New Bern in Craven County, Carteret County's Beaufort is the third oldest town in North Carolina, established in 1721. (And that's *Bo*-fort, with a long *o*, thank you very much; not *Bu*-fort like that other coastal town so far down the shores of South Carolina that it's almost in Georgia.)

For years our Beaufort was just a sleepy little fishing village on the Intracoastal Waterway. Then in the late seventies they tore down most of the ramshackle fish houses alongside Taylors Creek, rebuilt the piers, painted everything on Front Street in Williamsburg colors and now boats from all over the world—fishing boats, yachts, sailboats, even occasional tall ships—tie up at its docks and come ashore to drink in its bars and rummage through its self-consciously quaint shops.

Retirees have drifted in from all over, wealthy businessmen have built themselves second homes along the quiet coves and sheltered inlets, developers started calling our shoreline the Crystal Coast, and now tourism's a year-round industry.

Back away from the waterfront, the town itself hasn't changed all that much from what it was in my childhood except for the historical markers on more of the old white wooden houses. The courthouse still stands foursquare in a shady grove of live oaks a few blocks inland. It was built in 1907, red brick with tall white Doric columns on both its east- and south-facing porches. As with the old Colleton County courthouse back in Dobbs, modern courtrooms have been grafted onto the old building here and a new jail complex is rising out back.

A bailiff was waiting for me at the east porch. He gestured me toward an otherwise illegal parking space beneath one of the live oaks, took my briefcase and robe, and ushered me inside.

"Miz Leonard's office is down there on the right," he told me diplomatically.

Though she'd been elected on the Democratic ticket, Carteret's Clerk of Court wasn't terribly political and I knew her only by sight and reputation.

Her small reception room was empty; but as I approached the open inner door to her office, I was nearly knocked over by a short, very angry, barrel-shaped man. He pushed past with a muttered apology and I caught an expression of perplexed dismay on Darlene Leonard's face.

It changed to a warm smile as she stood to welcome me from behind a desk cluttered with manila folders, computer printouts, pictures of children and grandchildren, and a cut-glass vase of pansies. The office wasn't much wider than the desk, but tall windows stretched toward an even taller ceiling and lent a sense of spacious amplitude.

Things were slow enough back in Colleton County that when District Court Judge Roydon Mercer suddenly underwent emergency bypass heart surgery three days ago, my chief judge, F. Roger Longmire, volunteered me for a substitute. "They've never had a woman sit on a Beaufort bench," Roger said when he asked me to go. "Should be an interesting experience."

I forgot to ask him who was expected to find it interesting.

Evidently Darlene Leonard did.

"I've given you the judge's chamber that has its own private washroom." The sparkle in her eye announced an amused sensitivity to one of the biggest grumbles I hear from some of my male colleagues. They claim they're getting gun-shy about using any bathroom that has a connecting door because sometimes I forget to knock. We chatted a minute or two about inconsequentials—if she'd heard of the murder off Harkers Island, she didn't seem to connect it with me. Her assistant interrupted to say an expected phone call was on the line, and Mrs. Leonard said, "Now you be sure and let me know if there's anything you need."

I said I would.

Superior court was in session, too, the bailiff told me as we crossed into the modern section of the courthouse. "Insurance fraud. It'll probably go to the jury today."

In fact, I was zipping up my robe when Superior Court Judge Chester Amos Winberry tapped at my door and poked his head in without waiting for me to answer.

"What if I'd been standing here in my slip?" I asked sternly.

"I'd say when did you start wearing slips?" he grinned.

He had me there. I only own one: a black lace thing that keeps my black silk dress from clinging too tightly when I wear it to funerals; but I never thought anybody'd noticed the other times. Guess I'm going to have to start checking my silhouette against a brighter light.

Chet's a competent enough jurist. Some of us feel he goes a little too easy on white collar crime and a little too hard on blue collars, but that's not an unpopular mix down here. He's getting some gray now and the laugh lines no longer go away when he stops laughing; nevertheless, at fifty he's still a sexy man, knows it, and loves to act the cowboy. Most of the time, his wife, Barbara Jean, keeps him reined in; but she'll never break him from calling every female "darlin'," "honey," or "sugar."

"Heard you were down," he said. "Also heard you found Andy Bynum shot dead out by the banks. Are you okay?"

I nodded. "Did you know him?"

"Hell, everybody knew ol' Andy." He shook his head. "Bad, sad thing. Barbara Jean's all torn up about it. He was one of the few people that everybody listened to."

"About what?" I rummaged in my briefcase for a legal pad and a pen in case I needed to make notes to myself.

"About everything. How 'bout you recess at twelve sharp and let me and Barbara Jean take you out for some of the best she-crab soup you ever dipped a spoon in?"

"Can we cram that much lunch into an hour?"

"Oh, I always give my juries ninety minutes," he said magnanimously.

"Sounds about right to me," I told him.

We walked down a maze of short hallways and I entered the front of my courtroom from a door beside the bench.

"All rise," said the bailiff.

⌘

Most vehicular violations follow a predictable pattern across the state and Beaufort district court began no differently. There were the usual charges of speeding, driving under the influence, driving with suspended licenses, failure to wear a seat belt or to provide proper child restraints. (That last is something I take pretty seriously. It's one thing to risk your own life, but you don't want me on the bench if you're caught risking the life of a child.) One after another came calendared cases that could be duplicated from the mountains to the sandhills.

About mid-morning though, I hit something that could only occur at the coast: Felton Keith Bodie and James Gordon Bodie. Brothers. Twenty-two and nineteen, respectively. Charged with driving while intoxicated, impeding traffic, and unlawfully discharging a firearm to the public endangerment.

In simple English, according to the trooper who testified against them, he'd come across a small traffic jam off Highway 70, heading for Gloucester, shortly before midnight last Tuesday night. I'm familiar with that road and I know that stretches of it can get pretty dark and deserted. Too, there are deep drainage ditches on either side, so if anything blocks the road, it's hard to get by.

"Please describe to the court what you found," said the assistant district attorney.

"Well," said the trooper, referring to his notebook in a distinctive Down East accent, "these two were operating a 1986 F-150 Ford XL pickup. At the time I arrived on the scene, the pickup was skewed across the road and blocking traffic from both directions. Mr. Felton Bodie was trying to aim a spotlight mounted on the side of the truck and Mr. James Bodie was shooting at something on the edge of the road."

"And did you ascertain what their target might be?" asked the ADA.

"Well, I didn't have time to see anything at first, because as I was heading over to the driver's side of the truck, Mr. Felton Bodie yelled, 'You got him!' and then he jumped out of the truck and ran over to where Mr. James Bodie was wrestling something out of the ditch. They'd just got it th'owed in the back of the truck when I stepped around to the side where they were and asked them what was going on."

At that point, the trooper glanced at me and slipped into automatic pilot. "There was a strong odor of alcohol on and about the breath and persons of both suspects. Both were glassy-eyed, talkative, incoherent of speech, and unsteady of motion."

I nodded encouragingly and the ADA said, "Then what?"

"Then I relieved Mr. James Bodie of his rifle and took them both into custody."

"Did either defendant make a statement?"

"Mr. Felton Bodie said they were driving home to Gloucester when they saw an alligator on the side of the road and decided to shoot it. Mr. James Bodie said they were going to skin it out and sell the skin."

The two Bodie brothers sat at the defense table with egg-sucking looks of embarrassment on their faces.

Puzzled, I asked, "Aren't alligators protected?"

"Yes, ma'am, they sure are, Judge," said the ADA, waiting for me to step all the way in it.

I ran my finger down the calendar. "Are they being separately charged for that offense?"

"No, Your Honor," the trooper grinned. "'Cause it worn't a alligator they shot and put in the back of their truck. It was a four-foot retread off'n one of them big tractor-trailer tires."

I was laughing so hard I had to pick myself up off the floor before I could gavel everybody else in the courtroom back to order.

"Put up a big fight, did it?" I asked when the two Bodies rose to speak in their own defense.

In the end, I judged them guilty of a level five offense and gave them sixty days suspended, a hundred-dollar fine plus court costs, and twenty-four hours of community service as punishment for trying to shoot a protected species to the public endangerment. "And you'd just better be grateful there's no law against killing retreads," I told them.

Another dozen cases of speeding, failure to stop at stop signs or flashing red lights, unsafe movements, inspection violations, and driving without valid licenses carried us to twelve noon and lunch recess.

⌘

By 12:08 Chet and Barbara Jean Winberry and I were seated at a window table in the Ritchie House, a lovely old nineteenth-century building that had been refurbished and modernized so sensitively that it retained all its original charm and seaside grace. Despite the pricey rates, the guest suites on the second and third floor stayed booked year-round, and reservations were recommended for lunch and dinner both. Our table overlooked the marina, where several million dollars' worth of boats were moored. April sunlight sparkled off the water and glistened on gleaming white hulls and polished teak decks.

A waitress had brought our iced tea and a basket of hot and crisp hushpuppies as soon as we sat down, and Barbara Jean had already heard my account of finding her old colleague/ally/thorn in her side—I couldn't quite get an exact fix on their relationship, but maybe that was because she didn't seem to have one herself.

I've known and liked the Winberrys six or eight years even though they're both more than ten years older than me. Barbara Jean had inherited her family's menhaden fish-meal factory from her father; but she spent a lot of time running back and forth between Beaufort and Raleigh when Chet was appointed to a state commission during Governor Hardison's first term of office. The happiest day of their lives was when the governor appointed Chet a superior court judge down here in the First Division so they could both get out of Raleigh and come back to Beaufort to live full time.

There was a married daughter living on the western edge of Harkers Island and a baby grandson named for Barbara Jean's grandfather, the one who'd started the factory. Between all my older brothers and most of my friends, I've looked at an awful lot of baby pictures over the years.

This one was still in the tadpole stage, but when Barbara Jean and Chet both brought out their wallets, I made appropriate cooing noises.

The restaurant was light and airy, pale pink cloths and nosegays of sea oats graced the tables, white paddle ceiling fans circulated the air overhead. The few suits and ties in the room were worn by lawyer types. Everyone else seemed to have on canvas deckshoes, white duck or khaki pants, and pullovers or silky windbreakers that featured broad bands of turquoise or coral. Surely they couldn't *all* be sailing yachts back to Newport or Martha's Vineyard?

Several tables over were a handsome fortyish couple that could've stepped out of a Docksider ad. Between them, with her back to me, sat what looked like their daughter. Next to the woman, a little boy of two or three sat in a booster chair. All four had thick, straight blond hair. The man's was clipped short, as was the boy's; the woman's blunt cut brushed the shoulders of her white sweater, while the girl's long ponytail ended halfway down her back. Amusingly, the girl had brought along a hand puppet that was her twin in miniature: same long blonde ponytail, same coral-and-white nylon jumpsuit.

"Isn't she just precious?" agreed Barbara Jean, who'd followed my gaze. She bit into a crispy hushpuppy and said, "What'd you think of Jay Hadley?"

I cocked a cynical eye at Chet. "So now I'll ask her how she knows Jay Hadley and she'll tell me everybody down here knows Jay Hadley, right?"

"Well, most everybody who fishes for their livelihood." He gathered up the menus the waitress had handed us and said to her, "We're in sort of a hurry, darlin', so why don't you bring us each a nice bowl of your she-crab soup, then a big plate of lightly fried oysters and side dishes of slaw all around. That okay with you, Deborah? Honey?"

Barbara Jean and I agreed it sounded delicious to us.

Her roots go way back to Beaufort's beginnings, while Chet's people were carpetbaggers who came south after the Civil War. Even though Chet teases her that she married down, both are still more boardroom and resort town than leased bottoms and clam rakes, and it surprised me that she'd know Jay Hadley.

"Jay's real active in the Independent Fishers Alliance that Andy Bynum helped start. I'm a member, too."

"See, what's been happening down here," said Chet, "is that tempers have been getting more and more frayed these last few years."

"And with good cause," Barbara Jean chimed in.

"Everybody wants a slice of the resources and everybody thinks his wants are more justified than anyone else's."

"Well, some *are!*" Barbara Jean said hotly.

Chet grinned at me. "See? And she's one of the reasonable ones. Eat your soup, honey," he said as the waitress distributed wonderfully fragrant bowls of hot ambrosia.

She-crab soup is something like New England clam chowder, only made with the yellow roe and luscious back fins of female crabs.

Barbara Jean obediently savored a spoonful before diving back into a recitation of the area's conflicts.

"See, Deborah, for years the water here belonged to the people who worked it. We took out what we wanted, when we wanted, and as much as we wanted because fish and shellfish were plentiful and there weren't many rules or limits. Fishing was the backbone of Carteret County's economy. In fact, Beaufort was even called Fishtowne at one point. Then they started in with all the rules and regulations—"

"Because the water's overfished and varieties are declining," said Chet.

"For which we get all the blame. Never mind all the sportsmen coming down taking whatever *they* want, or developers destroying natural habitats, or the pier owners and the jet ski rentals and the tackle shop owners who don't want any nets or big boats in the sound because they say we're driving away the tourists. They particularly don't want any trawlers. You won't believe the propaganda they put out about us!"

I'd never seen her this vehement back in Raleigh.

"They're going to kill our menhaden industry. Thank God Chet's got a head for investments or we'd be out in the street. And what's going to happen to the men we employ? Twenty-three black families and—"

"And she's one of the reasonable ones?" I asked Chet.

"Maybe not as reasonable as Andy Bynum," he conceded as he reached for another hushpuppy.

"The government calls it protection and management of the resources," said Barbara Jean, "when it's nothing in the world but meddling and restrictive and economic murder."

"All the same," said Chet, "when the state started Marine Fisheries—"

"Marine Fisheries Commission," I murmured knowingly.

"—Andy made sure he was one of the commercial fishermen who got a seat on it. He was realistic enough to know that times really were a-changing. 'Regulations are coming,' he'd say, 'whether you want 'em or not.' And he figured he'd rather be on the inside helping to shape those regulations than on the outside watching commercial interests get swamped. Some of the watermen thought he was a traitor to their cause."

Barbara Jean nodded. "I was one of them at first. But some of what he had to say made sense. So many other interests are pulling at Core Sound now—developers, pier owners, the motels that cater to sportsmen, all those upstate surf fishers who say that trawling and netting interfere with their fun and then those Dare County millionaires with their pet legislators've got into it . . ." She shook her head in exasperation. "But Andy can—*could*—see all sides and most people on all sides would at least listen to him. I don't know who's going to take his place."

"Jay Hadley?" I asked.

Barbara Jean snorted. "A *woman?* Honey, you're talking the last bastion of male supremacy here. My daddy's been dead twelve years but they still call my company Wash Neville's plant."

I savored a final spoonful of soup. "The Hadley woman seemed pretty much in control when she came roaring out there yesterday with a .22 to see who was messing 'round their leased bottom. And what about that Alliance you mentioned?"

"Independent Fishers Alliance. That was Andy's idea. Most watermen work alone or in one- or two-man operations unless it's an established family business. I guess you'd call us a bit independent down here."

"Independent?" Chet shook his head as he began to divvy up the huge plate of oysters the waitress had set down in front of him. "Prickly as sea urchins and suspicious as hermit crabs."

"But Andy got us all together and gave us a coastal version of Abraham Lincoln," said Barbara Jean. "A boat divided against itself could not sail. United we might float, divided we'd surely drown. Jay Hadley did a lot of the secretarial work when it was getting started a few years back, and I think she still goes in a few times a week to pick up the slack when Andy's away. She's bright, Jay is. If she could've gone to college, no telling where she'd be now. Her husband started out like a lot of the old-timer proggers—"

"Proggers?" I'd occasionally heard the word over the years but never given it much thought.

"That's another of those Elizabethan remnants of speech," said Chet. "Means folks who forage around the water's edge, poking, or 'progging' at things."

Barbara Jean nodded. "That was Jay's husband all right—a traditional independent fisherman who thought he'd fish the cycle like his daddy and his granddaddy before him. It's taken her five years to convince Heston Hadley that leased bottoms could work, but she finally talked him into selling his big boat two years ago and putting the money into seed clams and mesh bags. They're going to make twice the money with half the effort if things keep going the way they have."

The oysters had arrived in sizzling perfection—crisp on the outside, plump and meltingly tender on the inside—and the next few minutes were devoted to a proper appreciation of Core Sound's continuing bounty.

"They're growing oysters on leased bottoms, too," Barbara Jean said between mouthfuls. "On ladders."

She was prepared to go into more details, but I didn't want to hear. "Will your Alliance continue without Bynum?"

She considered. "Who knows? Short-term? Maybe. Long-term? Till somebody's oars don't reach the water and Andy's not here to lift the ocean for them. Till all commercial fishing gets pushed slam out of the sound and off the banks, or the trawlers hear that they have to keep using turtle excluders and shrimpers don't. Jay can do the paperwork and maybe keep up with all the rules and regulations that keep rolling in till they can find some man to sit in Andy's chair, but finding someone that everybody trusts—"

Barbara Jean's words trailed off as her attention was diverted. I turned to see a stocky male stride through the crowded restaurant, jostling tables and diners and nearly causing a waitress to drop her tray. It was the same man who'd almost barreled me over at the Clerk of Court's office and he seemed even angrier now than he had earlier as he made his way over to a table halfway across the room from us.

It was occupied by a lone woman, another blonde (ash, this time), very petite, with oversized pale blue glasses that covered much of her face. Her hair fell in a loose pageboy along her chin line as she tilted her head toward the man, but her slender hand held its place in the papers she had been reading when he interrupted. No smile on her thin lips; no encouraging or conciliatory body language either. She sat absolutely motionless until he began to run out of steam, then turned back to her papers, clearly dismissing him.

He glared at her, thick hands on his hips, and anger deepened his voice. Everyone quit eating and flat-out stared.

"By God, I'll sue you for criminal fraud!" he shouted. "You knew I was going to turn it into a party boat."

She turned those pale blue glasses on him again. "You bought the *Lucky Linville* as is," she said calmly. "What you planned to do with her was not my concern."

She never raised her voice and if the room hadn't gone so silent, I wouldn't have been able to hear her. The manager and two hefty busboys surrounded the stocky man who by now was nearly apoplectic with rage.

As they hustled him out, the rest of us pretended we hadn't been staring. The woman returned to her reading completely unruffled. After an eternity, the usual flow of conversation ebbed back into the room with the tinkle of ice in tall glasses and the clink of utensils against china.

"She sold Zeke Myers the *Lucky Linville?*" Barbara Jean asked Chet just as I asked, "What was all that about?"

Chet shrugged, but suddenly I was remembering last night's phone call. "Is that Linville Pope by any chance?"

"You know her?"

"Not really. She invited me for cocktails tomorrow night. Said she was a friend of Judge Mercer's."

"I do hope you thought to pack a bulletproof vest," Barbara Jean said sweetly.

CHAPTER 4

Will your anchor hold in the storms of life,
When the clouds unfold their wings of strife?
When the strong tides lift and the cables strain,
Will your anchor drift, or firm remain?

—*Priscilla J. Owens*

With daylight saving now in effect, the sun was still high as I left the courthouse that afternoon and drove toward Harkers Island through a countryside less green than in other years. Only last month, a late-winter storm had left whole stretches of coastal pines, yaupon, azaleas, and live oaks so coated with salt spray that their needles and leaves had turned brown on the seaward side. Branches had shattered off and in more than one yard women were piling brush and men were still busy with chainsaws on trees uprooted by the storm.

Occasionally as I drove eastward, I spotted boarded-up windows, trailers that had shifted on their footings, and sheets of plastic tacked over gaping holes in the side of a house or roof.

For the first time, it belatedly registered just how much damage the coast had sustained. I remembered hearing radio bulletins that the "storm of the century" was headed our way, but then it had skipped over Dobbs and Raleigh so gently that I'd almost immediately quit paying attention.

True, Dwight Bryant, Colleton County's deputy sheriff, had done a lot of mouthing about the snows up in western Virginia (his ex-wife and young son lived in Shaysville and had been snowed in for several days), but late snows aren't uncommon in the Blue Ridge. If Channel 11's "Eyewitness" weatherman ever called it a hurricane—hurricanes in *March?*—I'm sure I'd have noticed; yet listening to Chet and Barbara Jean Winberry describe how the bottom seemed to have dropped out of their barometer, the ninety-miles-per-hour winds, gusting to over a hundred, what else could it have been?

At the courthouse, during our afternoon break, I heard of a nine-year-old killed when high winds snapped a pine over in Newport and sent it crashing into his family's mobile home. Roofs were ripped from houses, siding peeled from stores, sheets of tin had kited down the center of Morehead City.

"Lord, yes!" said one of the lawyers standing around the coffee urn. "Boats tore loose from moorings, the docks all along Taylors Creek were awash, and power lines?" He snapped his fingers. "Like two-pound test hit by marlins."

Much of the area was without electricity for more than a week, they told me, while power crews brought in from all over worked around the clock with local linesmen.

Somehow, it embarrassed me that I hadn't been aware of their ordeal, just as it bothered me that I hadn't known doodly about the issues that now inflamed Barbara Jean and others who earned their living from the ocean sounds and estuaries.

("You label the women of Harkers Island standoffish and aloof," lectured my internal preacher, *"yet when have you made more than self-serving perfunctory overtures?")*

Shamed, I thought about how I must look from their viewpoint. First as a child, then as a teenager, I'd come down with my cousins, played in the water, then gone juking and cruising around the Circle at Atlantic Beach. I treated their living space like a playground created for my personal pleasure. As an adult, I swam, water-skied, loafed, helped Carl and my younger cousin Scotty set gill nets out in front of the house so I could take home a couple of coolers of fresh seafood for my brothers and their families, then headed back inland to my comfortable life with less consideration than if those women were costumed characters in a theme park.

("Oh, give it a rest," fumed the cynical pragmatist, who usually starts jeering whenever I get any noble thoughts. *"You think anybody down here really feels deprived because one more upstater didn't try to be their best friend?")*

Okay, okay. Even so, just past Otway, I pulled in at a florist that was still open. The young woman behind the counter said she'd heard that Andy Bynum's body had been released to a funeral home on the island and that the funeral was scheduled for Wednesday afternoon. I ordered a basket of silk flowers to be sent: Dutch irises, buttercups, red poppies and lilies of the valley.

"Credit card friendship, the easiest kind," whispered a voice inside my head.

Preacher or pragmatist?

⌘

When I got back to the cottage, the Bynum house already had a closed-up look to it. His sons live further down the island, near the fish house, and I guessed the wake was probably being held at the funeral home.

I'd barely stepped through the door when the phone began ringing. Yeah, it could've been a dozen different people—I would even have welcomed somebody selling aluminum siding—but I had a feeling I wasn't going to be that lucky.

Actually, it could have been one of the mouthier ones. Could have been Andrew or Herman or Will or Jack. Instead, it was only Seth, five brothers up from me, and the brother who always cut me the most slack.

"Hey, Seth," I chirped. "You want me to bring you and Minnie some clams Friday?"

He didn't even bother to answer that. "What'd you go and get mixed up in now, Deb'rah?" he asked sternly.

At one time or another, most of my brothers had used this cottage or gone fishing with Carl, so Seth had met Andy and he listened without fussing as I explained the situation and how I was only tangentially involved. "How'd you hear so quick, anyhow?"

"Some SBI agent down there recognized your name and told Terry and Terry told Dwight and Dwight called me."

"I swear, you'd think SBI agents and deputy sheriffs would have better things to talk about. I hope nobody's worried Daddy with it."

"Not yet," Seth said. Concern was still in his voice. "You sure you haven't stepped in the middle of something, shug?"

I promised him that it was sheer coincidence and he promised that he'd do what he could to keep Daddy from hearing; and yeah, long as I was coming back Friday, a mess of clams might be right nice.

⌘

There was still no sign of Guthrie when I carried a glass of tea out to sit on the porch and unwind, but Mark Lewis and Makely Lawrence, two more of the neighboring youths, were headed up the path from the water, each with a bucket of clams they'd dug.

"You wouldn't want to sell me a half-dozen, would you?" I called.

Mark grinned. "No, but I'll give you six if that's all you want."

"I only want to make a small chowder."

"You give her three and I'll give her three," said Makely, not to be outdone by his cousin.

They set their buckets on the porch and each picked out their three biggest. The clams had been dug out of the mud, but they were the size of coffee saucers. As I should have suspected, the boys didn't want money, so much as they wanted details about Andy Bynum's death.

"Didn't Guthrie tell you?" I asked.

"Yeah, well—" said Makely.

"How come everybody says that?"

Makely looked at Mark, who said, "He got into trouble for taking his granddaddy's skiff out."

"What? I thought it was his."

"Ain't," Makely said tersely.

I let it pass and told them about going out with Guthrie, finding Andy lying dead, then Jay Hadley's arrival, followed by the police boat.

"Who do you think could have shot him?" I asked, curious to know what their elders were saying.

Again the shrugs.

"Drugs," Makely grunted. He was younger and almost as imaginative as Guthrie.

Mark was more thoughtful. "I don't know," he said slowly. "Lots of people were mad at him 'cause he was for making everybody buy a license to sell their fish. Like, if that happens, we wouldn't be supposed to sell you a mess of crabs or anything unless we had a license."

"Yeah," said Makely. "Heard tell shrimpers wanted to burn his house down."

"Just talk," said Mark, dismissively.

Perhaps. But as I was scrubbing the clams later, I thought about the island's reputation for settling its own scores. Even outsiders like me remembered the bitter anger and deep, deep hurt when Shackleford Banks was declared a wilderness area under the US Park Service.

Shackleford was the ancestral home of most islanders until the hurricanes of 1896 and 1899 forced them to relocate, and almost every island family maintained a rough fish camp over there. Unfortunately, few had clear deeds to the land. The two or three who did were given lifetime rights, but they fared no better than those with no deeds. When the untitled cabins were confiscated in 1985, some of the dispossessed went over and torched all the camps.

Had Andy Bynum angered some hot-tempered islander so thoroughly that a simple house-burning was not enough to settle the grudge?

⌘

The telephone rang as I finished gutting the clams and chopping them into small pieces. This time it was Carl, wanting to know if I found everything okay.

"Yeah, once Guthrie and I figured out your new water pump system."

"Same system it's always been," said Carl.

I sighed. "That Guthrie's got himself a reality problem, hasn't he?"

Carl laughed. "He been stretching the truth on you, too?"

He was startled to hear about Andy and I had to go through all the details again.

"Say it was out at Hes Hadley's leased bottom?"

There was a significant silence.

"What?" I asked.

It took some prodding, but eventually he repeated some gossip he'd heard from Mahlon Davis: "Said Hes warned Andy off his wife."

"Andy?" I was astonished.

"Oh, heck, yeah. Andy Bynum liked the ladies almost as much as Mahlon does. He just wasn't as crude about it."

He told me to be careful and not to go sticking my nose into anything that wasn't my business, a piece of advice every man in my whole family feels free to give, then he put Sue on so I could get her to go over the recipe for Core Sound cornmeal dumplings. ("One part plain flour to four parts cornmeal.")

"Did Andy ever make a pass at you?" I asked.

"Well, sure he did," she drawled. "I'd have been insulted if he hadn't, the way he used to flirt with every grown woman. Didn't mean anything. It was just his way of being polite. Now if it'd been Mahlon Davis . . ."

There was no need to elaborate.

She told me there was a little piece of salt pork in the freezer if I wanted it for my chowder and rang off without giving me any advice at all. Yet, paradoxically, it was her words that left me disoriented. Nothing sends you straight back to childhood quicker than getting an unexpected insight into how things—relationships—really were when you lived in Eden, a child oblivious to the Serpent.

⌘

While the clams simmered on the stove's lowest setting, I carried the shells and wastes down to dump at the water's edge. The fresh shell of a loggerhead turtle floated in the wash. Somebody not far away was probably enjoying a hot turtle stew at the moment—hot in more than one sense, because loggerheads are a protected species.

Almost twilight, yet gulls still came shrieking over, pushing and shoving and elbowing each other aside to be first at whatever was going down.

A line of brown pelicans flew by on their way to roost, as indifferent to the gulls as the sandpipers further down the sand.

Like their human counterparts, each had their own agenda for the water. Netters, tongers, dredgers or trawlers—according to Barbara Jean, the Alliance Andy Bynum had started wasn't so much a cooperative effort as a self-serving attempt to hang on to the particular niche each group considered a personal birthright.

Out in the channel, an expensive late-model sports boat headed for the Beaufort marina, and its running lights gleamed a rich red and green in the gathering dusk. A few moments later, its wake broke against the shore, scattering gulls and rocking the little homemade skiffs moored close in.

I turned and saw Mahlon's new trawler. More than half-finished now, it stood outside on blocks and dwarfed the small house. There was nothing sporty about it, but its lines were clean and solid, and the empty utilitarian cabin rose starkly against the dying light of the western sky.

And there was Mahlon himself, a gaunt wiry form half-hidden by the end post of his boat shed, standing motionless in the twilight as he stared at me. When he realized I'd seen him, he stepped forward. A caulk gun was in his hand and his fingers were coated with the yellow adhesive.

"Still like to feed the birds, do you?" His thick accent turned *like* to *loike*.

"How you doing, Mahlon?" I said, with more geniality than I felt.

"Just fair. Carl coming down?"

"Not this time."

"Ain't seen you down for a while. Staying long?"

"Just till the weekend."

He had to be over sixty now, and he'd lost weight since that shirt and work pants were new; but his corded forearms were still muscular and he still made me uneasy, Mahlon did. Only once had he ever acted out of the way with me and I'd never actually seen him hit his wife or deliver more than a casual swat to Guthrie's backside, yet I knew the violence his easygoing, laid-back exterior belied. His mother, Miss Nellie Em, seemed to be the only one who could face him down.

There were tales of monumental drunks, of neighbors' set nets deliberately torn or their boats rammed; his own boats wrecked through reckless misuse; and in the water straight out from his house, you could still see the last rusty remains of a car that had so angered him back in the early sixties that he'd driven it out as far as he could and then attacked it with his steel adze, smashing every piece of glass on the thing.

"Oi wore that mommicked," Mahlon would say whenever anyone asked him about it.

Men usually told these things with humorous zest and with the sneaking admiration a law-abider sometimes has for an outlaw.

Women were usually less amused.

Take that midsummer day. My cousins and I were thirteen or fourteen, and we were frolicking in the sound, enjoying our newly developing bodies, when Mahlon Davis staggered down to the shore on unsteady legs and stood on the sand to watch. For several minutes he swayed in the warm breeze and laughed to see us splash and dive and then erupt from the waves several yards away.

"Mermaids!" he suddenly bellowed. "Here's your king of the sea!" Next thing we knew, he was wading in to join us—fully dressed, leather shoes and all. We were astonished because we'd never seen an adult islander play in the water. He made a clumsy lunge for Carlette, who was the oldest and prettiest, but she easily eluded him; and his feet slid out from under him. He sat down up to his chest, then his head tilted backward and he was laughing so hard that we saw half-rotted teeth and gaps where several were already missing.

As one, we dived and swam away into deeper water until he finally staggered back to shore, retrieved the bottle he'd dropped on the sand, and disappeared around the corner of his house.

Later that evening, I had gone down alone to feed the gulls when I heard an incoherent roar of anger from inside his house. I heard Mahlon's wife cry, "No, don't!" Then the screen door flew open and a white cat slammed into the side of the new boat Mahlon was building and fell to the ground like a broken bottle of bloody champagne.

Horrified, I fled back to the cottage.

Yet when he was sober, his skill fascinated me.

He might not be the equal of Brady Lewis, great-grandfather to both young Mark Lewis and Makely Lawrence and a boat builder of undisputed genius—he originated the unique Harkers Island flared bow—but Mahlon Davis was still a skilled craftsman.

When he wanted to be.

Trouble was, most of the time he didn't want to work that steadily.

I looked at the keel of the forty-foot trawler he was building now. Hundreds of pieces of juniper wood, two inches wide, no two curved exactly the same, yet each edge lay snugly against the other, nailed on the face to the heart pine ribs and again through the edge.

Mahlon's lot was too narrow to accommodate house, boat shed and a boat this big and still have room to maneuver, so he'd hacked away some of the weedy trees that covered the property west of his. Mickey Mantle's cockerel pens were already there—each wire cage held a feisty-eyed bantam rooster, and now the trawler's bow extended eight or ten feet into the clearing.

"You're working late," I observed.

"Just caulking. Don't need daylight for that." He turned back with the caulk gun. A bare low-wattage light bulb hung next to the side where he was carefully waterproofing each nail head.

I followed, unable to resist the lure of watching something so beautiful and so practical take shape under his rough hands. No blueprints hung from the back wall of the shelter, not even any photographs. He didn't need a drawing to look at; it was all in his head. If I scrabbled around through the scraps of juniper, I might find a board with two columns of numbers scribbled on it, one for the dead rise and the other for the center, each figure accurate to the thirty-second of an inch so that she'd ride centered and true as long as she was cared for.

"Who you building this one for?" I asked.

"Me. Me'n my boys." He dotted a row of nail heads with the yellow caulk, then smoothed each dot with his fingers. "I hear tell you're a judge now."

"Yes."

"Tell me this, if you would. Say somebody didn't like my mess on their property. Can they have it all hauled off and make me pay for it?"

"Somebody doing that to you?"

"Yeah, some bitch over to Beaufort that bought that field." He nodded toward the overgrown, debris-littered field. His debris. Behind the chicken cages, there was a broken-down pickup full of junk that'd been there at least eight years. Sticking up from the scrubby bushes were piles of building scraps, aluminum siding, and old pipes and barrels. Further out, a yaupon tree grew straight up through a cast-off stove.

"She says if I don't get my mess off, she'll pay somebody twenty-five hundred dollars and put the law on me if I don't pay it. I ain't got twenty-five hundred dollars. This boat's taking every penny and I still got to get the diesel engine for her. Andy was going to let me have one off a old truck of his, but now, I don't know if his boys'll still do it or not."

"Well, she can't have you hauled off to jail like a criminal," I assured him, "but she could file in civil court and get a judgment against you."

"What would that mean?"

"It might mean a forced sale of your house if you didn't pay up after a certain length of time."

"I knew it!" he said angrily. "That's what she's after. She's already got title to two or three pieces along here. If she'n get mine and maybe Carl's—"

"Carl and Sue would never sell," I said.

"It ain't been in his family a hundred years," Mahlon said shortly. "Wave enough money under people's noses and you can't tell what they'd do."

He smoothed on some more caulk dots. "Well, it don't signify. With this boat, me'n my boys're gonna get ourselves out'n the hole for good and all this time."

"How *is* Mickey Mantle?" None of us ever knew whether or not to ask, but since Mahlon had mentioned him first . . .

His sun-leathered face crinkled with a gap-toothed grin. "Doing a lot of walking these days."

"Oh?"

He smoothed another row of nail heads. "Yeah. Got his license pulled again. For a year this time. If he can't get there by boat or thumb, he has to foot it."

"So you figure that'll keep his mind on fishing for a while?" I laughed.

"Should do," he answered dryly. "If I'n get her done by the time shrimping season starts, the money'll keep 'em both in line."

I hesitated. "I hope I didn't get Guthrie in trouble yesterday, asking him to take me out for clams?"

Mahlon scowled. "Worn't your fault. He knowed better'n to take my skiff 'thout asking."

"That was pretty awful about Andy Bynum getting shot."

"Yeah." He laid aside the caulk gun and began to peel the gummy stuff from his fingers.

"I guess you're in that Alliance he started?"

"Hell, no!" He saw my puzzlement. "Oh, they tried to sign us all up, but I ain't never joined nothing yet and I'm sure not gonna start with something that don't give a damn about me."

"But I thought it was to help the independent fishermen."

He snorted. "Yeah, that's what was *said,* but I ain't never seen nothing started by the man that don't end up with money in their pockets."

Startled, I tried to remember if I'd ever seen Andy linger under Mahlon's boat shed or seen Mahlon over at Andy's. "You and Andy weren't friends?" I asked.

"He was the man," he said, as if that explained it all.

Well, if Andy was, I guess it did, diesel engine or no diesel engine.

Mahlon wrapped a piece of plastic around the tip of the caulk gun, secured it with a rubber band, then reached over and turned off the light bulb.

"Reckon I'd better get on in to eat," he said, reminding me of the chowder I'd left simmering on the stove.

It was full dark but there were enough scattered lights from nearby houses to guide me the few feet down the shoreline to the main path once my eyes adjusted. I went slowly, thinking about "the man." Not a purely local concept, of course. There was that old Ernie Ford coal miner song about owing one's soul to the company store. And sharecroppers certainly knew about never getting out of debt to the man who bankrolled you to the tools or supplies you needed if you were going to work for him.

Andy Bynum had owned a fish house. Barbara Jean could probably tell me exactly how that made him the man.

As I headed up the path to the cottage, the maniacal cry of a migrant loon rang across the sound.

CHAPTER 5

We are waiting by the river,
We are watching by the shore,
Only waiting for the boatman,
Soon he'll come to bear us o'er.
Though the mist hang o'er the river,
And its billows loudly roar,
Yet we hear the song of angels,
Wafted from the other shore.

—Miss Mary P. Griffin

Tuesday's court began slowly as we finished off the traffic violations and moved on to various misdemeanors (which I could hear) and some extra probable-cause felonies (which would have to be bucked up the next level to superior court).

Despite Mahlon's optimistic talk, I wasn't terribly surprised when a familiar figure came up to the defense table and signed the form waiving his rights to an attorney.

Mickey Mantle Davis.

According to the ADA, he sat accused of stealing a bicycle from the deck of the *Rainmaker,* a forty-footer out of Boston, currently berthed at the dock on Front Street. The state was hoping to prove probable cause to prosecute as a felony burglary.

"How do you plead?" I asked.

He stood up with a happy smile because he had just recognized me. "Not guilty, Judge, ma'am."

Technically, I could have recused myself right then and there, but Mickey Mantle Davis would've had to go over to one of the piedmont or mountain districts to find a judge that hadn't heard of him. From the time he was fourteen and buying beer with a stolen driver's license, Guthrie's father has been smashing up cars and smashing up boats and smashing up every second chance people still try to give him because shiftless as he is, he's still a likeable cuss. He'd work hard for a week, then lay out drinking for two weeks; steal your portable TV on Friday night, then bring you a bushel of oysters on Saturday—a walking cliché of the good-hearted, good-timing wastrel who had so far managed to stay, if not out of trouble, at least out of a penitentiary.

Good luck to Mahlon keeping him on a trawler the whole of shrimping season.

"Call your first witness," I told the ADA.

A Beaufort police officer took the stand and, after my recording clerk swore him in, testified how the dispatcher had radioed a description of both the bike and the thief. Within the hour, he'd seen the defendant pedaling such a bike toward the Grayden Paul drawbridge, heading for Morehead City. Upon being stopped and questioned, Mr. Davis had claimed that he'd found the bike by the side of the road and was taking it over to Morehead City to put a found ad in the *Carteret County News-Times*.

"No further questions," the ADA said dryly.

"Me neither," said Mickey Mantle.

"Call Claire Montgomery," said the ADA.

On the bench behind him sat the three fashion plates I'd noticed at lunch the day before. Claire Montgomery was evidently the blonde pony tailed youngster. As she took the witness box, hand puppet and all, I was surprised to see that she wasn't the eleven- or twelve-year-old I'd originally assumed, but at least nineteen or twenty. I was so busy shifting mental gears that the clerk had almost finished administering the oath before I registered that it wasn't—strictly speaking—Claire Montgomery's hand which lay on the Bible held up by the bailiff. Instead, her hand was inside the doll's body and she manipulated it so that the puppet raised its right hand and touched the Bible with its left. Although the young woman's lips moved, I assume it was the puppet's voice that swore to tell the truth, the whole truth and nothing but the truth.

"State your name and address," said the ADA.

The puppet gave me a courteous nod and seemed to say, "Our name is Claire Montgomery and we live at Two-Oh-Seven—"

"Just a minute, Miss Montgomery," I interrupted. "This is a serious court of law, not a vaudeville stage. I must ask you to put aside the doll."

"But we saw him take our bicycle," the puppet protested. Its long blonde ponytail flounced impatiently.

The girl looked only at the puppet, the puppet looked only at me. The girl was so still (except for her lips), the puppet so animated that for an instant, I almost started to argue with the small plastic face—the illusion was that good. Claire Montgomery might not be a ventriloquist, but she was a damn fine puppeteer.

"Nevertheless, a man is on trial here," I said sternly.

"The doll don't bother me none," said Mickey Mantle Davis from the defense table.

I beckoned to the ADA, who approached with studied nonchalance. When his head was close enough to mine, I whispered, "Am I the only one who sees something strange about a puppet giving testimony? What the hell's going on?"

The ADA, Hollis Whitbread, was a nephew of "Big Ed" Whitbread back up in Widdington, and he didn't seem to have much more smarts than his uncle. He gave a palms-up shrug and muttered. "That's her sister and brother-in-law on the front row."

I glanced over. Mr. and Mrs. Docksider were accompanied by a man in jeans and blue blazer who sported a neatly trimmed salt-and-pepper beard.

"She says the girl had some sort of trauma in childhood and ever since, she'll only talk to strangers through the puppet. If you take the puppet away, she'll just shut down entirely, and since she's the only one that saw Davis take the bicycle . . ."

I sighed. "The puppet talks or he walks?"

"You got it, Judge."

The puppet was a perfect witness, respectful, charming, articulate, with an eye for details. I've been in court when molested children used dolls to help describe what had been done to them; this was the first time I'd heard a doll testify on its own. It was, to borrow Barbara Jean Winberry's term, just precious; and the entire courtroom, Mickey Mantle included, hung on every word as the puppet described resting in Claire Montgomery's bunk on the *Rainmaker* while her young nephew napped on the bunk below. They were alone on the boat. Her sister, Catherine Llewellyn, and the rest of their party had gone ashore.

The bike, a two-hundred-dollar all-terrain workhorse, was racked in its own locker on the starboard deck directly beneath Miss Montgomery's gauze-curtained window and she had a perfect view when a man crept on board, jimmied the lock with his pocket knife, and stole the bike.

"Do you see the man who stole the bike in this courtroom?" asked the ADA dramatically.

Without hesitation, the puppet pointed to Mickey Mantle Davis.

"No further questions," said Hollis Whitbread.

"Mr. Davis, you are not obliged to—"

Mickey Mantle was grinning ear to ear. "Oh, I *want* to, Judge."

I bet he did.

Hugely enjoying himself, the sorry scoundrel tried to browbeat the puppet into admitting it'd seen someone else, not him.

The puppet tossed its ponytail and refused to back down.

After the second "Did, too," "Did not!", I'd heard enough.

Modern statutes have expanded the common law definition of burglary to include boats as a dwelling. By proving Davis had trespassed onto the *Rainmaker*, then broken into and "entered" the bike locker, Whitbread hoped to stretch a misdemeanor theft to a felony burglary and finally get Mickey Mantle put away for some real time.

"Sorry, Mr. Whitbread," I had to say. "But I find no probable cause for remanding this case to superior court. Even with a credible witness, you're on shaky ground with only a bike locker as your B and E, and I cannot in good conscience accept this witness. Without corroboration, it's Davis's word against the officer's that he was heading for the paper and not a pawnshop. Case dismissed."

"Hey," said Mickey Mantle. "Do I get a reward for finding their bicycle?"

Claire Montgomery gave me a disgusted glare, the first direct meeting of our eyes; then she and her party left the courtroom.

Already, my attention was turning to the next case when something only peripherally seen abruptly jarred a nerve. I peered at the swinging doors. Too late. The *Rainmaker* crew were gone. Now why should their departure suddenly conjure up kaleidoscopic images of New York?

"Line twenty-seven on the add-on calendar, Your Honor. Taking migratory birds without a valid permit," said Hollis Whitbread, and reluctantly I pushed down memories of pastrami sandwiches four inches thick. Cappuccino on the Upper West Side. Columbia's gray stone buildings . . .

What—?

"The State calls—," Hollis Whitbread droned, and I dragged my thoughts back five hundred miles to this Carteret County courtroom.

⌘

During the lunch recess (limited to forty-five minutes to make up for yesterday), I walked out the back door of the courthouse and down a rough plank walkway to the sheriff's office, trying to avoid the mud and construction rubble. The taxpayers of Carteret County weren't building their new jail house a minute too soon if this poorly lighted warren of tiny cramped offices reflected the condition of the old cells.

"The sheriff's at lunch," said the gray-haired uniformed officer on desk duty when I explained why I'd come. "Want me to see if Detective Smith's in?"

I nodded and she punched a button on her outdated phone console. "Hey, sweetie, Quig still there? Judge Knott's here to sign her statement. 'Bout finding Andy Bynum? Okey-dokey."

She smiled up at me. "You can go on across."

"Across?"

Turning to follow her pointing finger, I looked through the glass of the outer door and saw a house trailer parked at the edge of the muddy yard. The aluminum door opened and Detective Quig Smith gave me a big come-on-over wave.

Smith was about four inches taller than my five six. Mid-fifties. If he had any gray in that thatch of hair, it was disguised by sun-bleached blond. His eyes were a deep blue, the shade of weathered Levis. And he seemed to be one of the more talkative Down Easters, greeting me like an old friend after our one meeting out in the sound over Andy Bynum's body.

I was ushered into the modular cubicle that functioned as his temporary office till they could move into new quarters, "Though Lord knows if it'll happen before I retire."

I politely murmured that he didn't look old enough to retire, and in truth he didn't.

"Thirty years the fifth of November and then I'm outta here," he said cheerfully as he riffled through files looking for my statement. "Gonna become the biggest, meanest, peskiest mosquito the state of North Carolina ever had whining around their ears."

"Oh?"

"Yep. Gonna be another full-time watchdog for the Clean Water Act. I've already loaded my computer with the name and address of every elected official in this voting district, everybody on relevant congressional committees, and every newspaper in the state with a circulation over five thousand."

He lifted a stack of marine conservation magazines from his desk and added them to a heap growing on the floor beside his file cabinet.

"Every time we find a violation of federal rules, they're gonna get a letter giving time, date, location, and nature of the violation. Gonna keep score of how they respond, too. Got a nephew taking computer courses over at Carteret Community College and he's writing me up my own special program. Now where did I put—"

It looked to be a lengthy search. From the only half-empty chair available, I removed a printout labeled *North Carolina Fishery Products* and sat down.

"Guess you're for regulating the fishing industry, too, then," I said, wondering how he ever managed to find anything in this overflowing wastebasket that masqueraded as an office.

"Not particularly." He opened a folder, frowned at its contents, and stuck it back in the heap. "Fishermen are a lot more realistic about managing resources than landsmen and what they take out of the sound doesn't begin to touch what more people inland do to the estuarine nurseries where so much of marine life begins. Some municipal sewage systems are so outdated that they dump twice as much untreated waste in the rivers as they do treated. Then there's the phosphate factories, the pesticides and fertilizers from farms, the runoff from parking lots, developers cutting finger canals into the wetlands so every condo in every retirement village can have its own boat landing and—ah! Here it is."

He handed over a one-page statement which I read and signed.

"Any progress on finding Andy's killer?" I asked, using the prerogative of position to interrupt his environmental monologue. "Or why he was killed?"

Quig Smith shook his head. "We keep asking around, of course, trying to piece together who else was out there around midday."

"That's when he was killed?"

"Between twelve and one, looks like, according to stomach contents. He had a Coke and Nabs at Cab's around ten-thirty or eleven. They say he made a phone call and kept checking his watch before he left. We reckon if he went straight from the store, he was probably out on the shoal by noon. Jay Hadley saw him there around twelve-thirty. After that—" He shrugged.

"Trouble is, it was Sunday. Lot of fishermen go to church, lot of sportsmen—strangers—head out through the channel that nobody ever saw before. And most people that live down here and have a boat, they'd have their own landing to go and come from."

"What about motive?"

"Most people don't get to be sixty without making a few enemies," Smith said vaguely.

"Was it something to do with his fish house, or because of the Alliance? Or was it personal?" I persisted.

Smith rubbed his chin. "Well, you know, Judge, down here, messing with a man's living's about as personal as messing with his wife."

"And you don't plan to tell me a damn thing, do you?"

I smiled to show I wasn't taking it personally and he rubbed his chin some more, then said, "We got somebody to come out with a underwater metal detector after you and Jay Hadley left."

"Oh?"

"Well, I got to thinking how you said you and the Davis boy turned the body straight over without shifting it. So, figuring he fell straight forward, we did some measuring and some angle projections and we got lucky. 'Long with some old rusty nails and a real nice little anchor, we found a new-looking slug. Sent it up to Raleigh to see what the SBI lab can tell us about it. Looked like a .22 to me, which won't be a lot of help 'cause half the county's bought a .22 at one point or another and the other half's stolen one or two."

"Jay Hadley had a .22 in her boat," I reminded him.

"Yeah. And somebody said they saw her shoot a gun while y'all were out there."

Lots of binoculars had probably swept the area once she'd radioed for help, so it didn't surprise me to hear that we'd been observed. Nor to realize that Smith wanted to hear about the incident.

"She said she saw a stingray."

"Yeah?"

"Guess it'd make as good a reason as any if you were scared some hotshot lawman might notice you had a recently fired rifle on your boat," I said blandly.

He laughed. "Maybe I ought to sign you up to be a mosquito, too."

⌘

Afternoon court was more wildlife violations (the hunting season for tundra swans was long over and loons haven't been in season since 1919). Worthless checks, minor drug possessions and an obscene phone caller carried us up to adjournment. At the recess, Chet Winberry knocked on my door while I was signing a show cause order for one of the attorneys.

"Don't let me interrupt," he said. "Linville's invited us to her party, too, and Barbara Jean said if you want to come by after court and freshen up at our place, we could go on over together."

It was a welcome invitation. I'd stuck a garment bag with party clothes in my car that morning, and this would save me having to change in chambers and then figure out exactly where Linville Pope lived.

Chet adjourned his court earlier than mine, but he'd sketched a map and sent it down with his clerk. The directions looked simple enough: straight east on Front Street till you almost ran out of land at Lennox Point, which was less than two miles across North River Channel from Harkers Island as the gull flies.

I'd been to parties at the Winberrys' house in North Raleigh when he was still an attorney with the state and they were alternating weekends back and forth from Beaufort, but this was a first for down here.

After passing Live Oak Street, a main artery back to Highway 70, Front Street meanders on down along Taylors Creek, so close to Carrot Island that you can see the famous wild ponies grazing its sparse vegetation. At the town limit, Front makes a sharp left turn and dead ends into Lennoxville Road right at Beaufort Fishery, a collection of tin-sided buildings inside a chain-link fence. Moored out front was a large trawler, the *Coastal Mariner*. Somewhat further on down, but less than half the size, was Neville Fishery, the only other menhaden factory still left on the coast of North Carolina. The trawler anchored there was much smaller. Rustier, too.

I drove slowly, enjoying the views that opened between ancient moss-draped live oaks. As a kid, I'd often taken Spanish moss home from the coast and draped it on our own trees, but our inland air is too dry and it never wintered over. To my left, azaleas flamed around the foundations of spacious houses set back from the road. To my right, Carrot Island stood out crisply in the April sunlight, and I rolled down my windows so I could enjoy the cool salty air.

Eventually I passed a landmark on Chet's map and started counting mailboxes till I came to one that serviced a nearly unnoticeable lane that curved off through yaupon, myrtle and scrub pines. Once through the wall of shrubbery, I saw an attractive low white brick house that spread itself modestly in its own grove of shady live oaks. Beds of red, pink and white azaleas interplanted with tulips and white ageratum wound extravagantly through the grounds. All in all, except for the boat dock out back and the water beyond that, it wasn't so very different from their North Raleigh house.

Barbara Jean met me at the door, still in jeans and sweatshirt, with a familiar smell of fish in her hair. She handed me a light-on-the-bourbon and Pepsi, just the way I like it, and insisted on taking my garment bag. We went straight down a wide hall and into a spare bedroom, Barbara Jean talking the whole way.

"Have you talked to Quig Smith? Are they any closer to finding who killed Andy?"

"Not that he's saying," I told her. "He was killed with a .22 and Smith says everybody down here has one."

"Not us," said Chet from the doorway of their bedroom. "Not any-more." He gestured toward an empty gun case at the other end of the hall. "Somebody jimmied the lock last week and took all four of our guns, including the .22 my dad gave me when I was twelve."

"And we need to file an insurance claim on them, too, hon," said Barbara Jean as she laid my bag across a comforter patterned in bright daffodils. "I should have told you to spend the night, Deborah, instead of making that drive back to Harkers Island. Why don't you? Then you won't have to worry about how many drinks you have. I can lend you a toothbrush and nightgown. No trouble."

"Just how late do cocktail parties last down here?" I asked curiously.

"Anywhere from two hours to two days," said Chet.

He'd already showered and dressed and looked exceedingly hand-some in his navy blazer and pale gray slacks. Barbara Jean told him so and he leered back at her.

Barbara Jean was taller than me, with good facial bone structure, nice legs and a figure well worth a spare leer or two, even in her work clothes.

For a moment, they reminded me of my brother Seth and his wife Minnie. Must be nice to be a grandmother and still have a husband look at you that way.

She showed me towels and hair dryer, then went off to bathe while Chet trailed along. "To help," he explained.

The Winberrys were not what you'd call wealthy—the bulk of Chet's practice had been Neville Fishery before his appointment to that state commission, and Barbara Jean's little fish meal factory probably didn't net her much more than Chet's salary these days. I gathered it had been quite profitable all during her childhood, however, and family investments allowed her and Chet to raise their only daughter in comfortable luxury.

This had been the daughter's bedroom and the adjoining shower had pale yellow tiles, each hand-painted with a single spring flower and no two alike, so that it took me longer to look at each tile than it did to wash my hair and bathe.

Another five minutes with towels and blow dryer, then I slipped into a cream-colored silk jumpsuit that did good things for my hair and skin. Body lotion, makeup, chains of crystals and pearls to soften the tailored shirt top, more crystals for my ears; finally a flat Mexican purse woven of turquoise and red and gold to add a touch of color.

"Very nice," Chet said appreciatively, but it was clearly Barbara Jean who delighted him more. Her short navy-blue dress had long skintight sleeves. Cut high in front to accent a string of antique pearls, its low back revealed skin that was still smooth and supple.

Chet was tall, yet Barbara Jean topped his shoulders in her high heels as they led the way down to their boat landing. He pulled her close and I heard him murmur, "That the perfume I bought you last week?"

When she nodded, he smiled back at me. "Old lady looks pretty good to've cooked up a half-million fish today, doesn't she?"

"Is that what she did?" As we walked along their dock, I was trying not to catch a spike heel in the cracks between the wide, salt-treated planks.

"Well, not in my kitchen," she said dryly. "But yeah, the *Washington Neville* brought in its largest haul of the season today. Let's just hope the wind doesn't shift till after Linville Pope's party. The smell of cooking menhaden smells like jobs and income to most of us, but it stinks to her. She'd rather see our black workers on welfare or fetching and carrying for the white tourists."

"Now honey," said Chet as he handed us into the stern of their rakish inboard speedboat. "You promised to be nice tonight."

"I promised not to spit in Linville's face," she grinned. "Nothing was said about being nice."

"Fireworks?" I said hopefully, leaning forward from my seat behind them. "Drinks tossed? Fistfights? Hairpulling?"

"Not by me." Barbara Jean parodied ladylike virtue. "My factory is sitting in the middle of some choice waterfront property that Linville's dying to develop, but you won't hear *me* bring up the subject."

Chet started the motor with a moderate roar that immediately leveled off to a quietly expensive purr as we slid gently away from the landing dock. The low sun shafted beams of gold up through bands of mauve and blue-gray clouds. The wind was so light it barely ruffled our hair and Chet kept our speed just above a fast walk as we rounded the point and headed northwest.

"So brief me about Linville Pope," I said. "Other than the fact that you don't like her, what else should I know to keep me from putting my foot in my mouth?"

"You want the chamber of commerce gloss or to back of Rose's dirt?"

"Oh, the catty version, by all means."

"Trailer trash from Cherry Point," she said flatly.

Seated behind the wheel, Chet laughed and reached out a hand to tousle her blonde curls. "Deb'rah said catty, honey, not bitchy."

She considered. "Okay, maybe not trailer trash, but her father was career military—some say a staff sergeant; *she* says a light colonel—and when he was reassigned, she was a junior at East Carolina, so she stayed behind. She'd already got her hooks into Midge Pope by then. He inherited a broken-down old motel over at Atlantic Beach and after they married, she got a broker's license and used the motel to leverage the Ritchie House. Now she's got about six agents working for her and Pope Properties handles some of the priciest real estate in the area."

"I'm impressed. The Ritchie House must have a license to mint money."

"Yeah, well Chet tried to talk old Mr. Janson out of selling it so cheaply, but she sweet-talked her way past him."

She looked at Chet. "What else?"

"Hinges on her heels?" he suggested, as a string of brown pelicans crossed our bow.

"Oh God, yes! All a man has to do is touch her and over she goes. I'll say one thing for her though. At least she's not dumb enough to shit up her own landing."

"That means she doesn't mess around with any local married men," Chet translated. He gave an exaggerated sigh. "Lord knows I've tried to change her mind often enough."

We laughed.

"Where's her husband in all this?"

"Midge? Drying out again near Asheville last I heard. She's after some Jew-boy right now. A Boston lawyer, is it, hon?"

Chet caught my expression and Barbara Jean caught his.

She twisted around in her seat. "Deborah knows I don't mean anything ugly by that, don't you, Deborah? If Midge Pope never cared who or what his wife screwed, why should I? But this new guy *is* Jewish and he *is* from Boston, so what's wrong with saying it?"

"Long as some of your best friends are black," I said wryly.

I don't think she got it because she started talking about someone named Shirl Kushner.

Even so, it was lovely to slip along the shoreline like this. The slap of water against our hull, the snap of the ensign in the stern, and the cry of gulls all around exaggerated the differences, but for a moment I was reminded of being on a train, slicing through backyards and alleyways usually hidden from view. Had we been driving through the street along this same stretch of land, we'd have glimpsed only the public facade masked by live oaks and yaupon, not these wide terraces, lush flower gardens, and sturdy docks with some sort of water craft tied up at each.

For some reason, I'd assumed that Linville Pope lived over in Morehead. Instead, it seemed we'd barely gotten onto the water good until Chet was putting in at a long private pier with white plank railings. Other boats were there before us and several hands reached out to take the line Chet threw and to help us step onto the dock when the line was secured.

More people spilled across the broad flagstoned terrace that began at the end of the planked walk. Everyone greeted Chet and Barbara Jean, and names and faces blurred as my friends rattled off introductions.

One elderly white-haired lady—"Miss Louisa Ferncliff, this is Judge Knott"—grasped my arm dramatically. "My dear, how on earth could you manage to sit in court after such a horrible, horrible experience?"

She made it sound like a breach of good taste that I hadn't gotten the vapors from finding Andy Bynum's body. I smiled vaguely and trundled after Barbara Jean.

Two white-jacketed black men were passing trays of white wine or taking drink orders and the older one spoke warmly to Barbara Jean. She seemed genuinely pleased to see him, too.

"Deborah, meet Micah Smith," she said. "He was one of the chanteymen when my daddy first took over. Helped pull the nets before everything went hydraulic, then helped with the cooking till he retired last year. He said he was going to sit on a dock and fish the rest of his life."

"Pleasure to meet you, ma'am," he told me. "And I found out fishing every day quits being fun when you *can* fish every day. Now I he'p Miz Pope when she gives parties. And what can I fetch you two pretty ladies tonight?"

I opted for a Bloody Mary since I hadn't eaten anything except an English muffin for breakfast and a cone of frozen yogurt at lunchtime. Barbara Jean wanted a margarita. "And where's our hostess, Micah? Judge Knott hasn't met her yet."

He pointed toward a set of open French doors that led into the house. "She's in yonder."

"Come on, Deborah. We'll go make nice and then I'll introduce you to one of the richest and hunkiest bachelors here. You like to marlin fish? You should see some of those million-dollar boats up close."

Without waiting for an answer, she hauled me through the crowd and only laughed when I muttered, "If this is just a few friends over for drinks, what constitutes a real party?"

⌘

Drink in hand, Linville Pope stood facing us as we entered the long living room, but her attention seemed totally focused on the man to whom she was speaking. I remembered how still she'd sat in the restaurant yesterday when accosted by that angry shouter. An unusual ability, this knack she had of centering a pool of stillness and silence around her small body.

"How nice you could come," she said when Barbara Jean had introduced us. "I didn't realize when we spoke Sunday night that you'd been involved with Andy Bynum's death. How awful for you."

I barely heard because her companion turned and it was the same man who'd sat in court this morning with the Llewellyns, the couple who were related to the puppeteer. Not much taller than me, he had short wiry hair which was flecked with gray, as was his neatly clipped beard.

I suddenly felt as if someone had knocked the wind out of me as Linville Pope said, "And this is Levi Schuster. I believe you two have met before?"

Lev smiled and said, "Hello, Red. So. Don't I get a kiss for old times' sake?"

CHAPTER 6

Jesus calls us o'er the tumult
Of our life's wild, restless seas . . .
In our joys and in our sorrows,
Days of toil and hours of ease.

—*Mrs. Cecil F. Alexander*

"Red?" asked Barbara Jean. "But she's a blonde." She gave my hair a critical look. "Sort of. Sandy anyhow. So why Red?"

You'd have to be thicker than a creosoted piling not to sense the waves cresting around us, and Barbara Jean's not thick.

Her question gave me time to find breath enough to steady my voice—I think it was steady—before I took his outstretched hand and said, "Hello, Lev."

"It's short for Redneck," Lev told Barbara Jean. My hand was swallowed up in his. I'd forgotten how big his hands were. He was only one and three-fourths inches taller than me, yet each hand would make almost two of mine. Hands that had picked me up when I slipped on those icy steps, hands that later pulled me down upon him, hands that guided my—

("Enough of that now!" warned the preacher.)

Abruptly, I pulled my hand free.

"Redneck?" Linville Pope was prepared to be amused. "I am sure there is a story here."

"She was the only one in my ethics class," he explained.

"Lev was a graduate assistant when I was in law school at Columbia," I said. "And redneck wasn't the only category I filled." I was back in control now and glibly prepared to amuse. "I forget exactly what the point of it was—demographics maybe, or the insularity of urban ethnicity—anyhow, this was one of those huge lecture sessions when Lev was subbing for the professor. He asked everybody who was Jewish to raise a hand and about two-thirds of the class did. Then he asked all the Catholics and another third of the hands went up. Then he asked for all the

Protestants and four hands went up: me, one black guy, and two Asians, which meant I was the only WASP as well."

"So never having seen that many WASPs up close, I naturally made her stay after the class," Lev said, bending the truth like one of his Aunt Ida's homemade pretzels. "And here she is, a judge."

"And here *you* are, a—what are you now, Lev?"

"A potential investor in a very nice project I am putting together," Linville Pope said smoothly.

"If the details can be worked out," he agreed, looking at me with half-tilted head.

"But not tonight," said Linville Pope. "Not now that you have found an old . . . student?"

She must know him well, I thought, to pick up on that undercurrent in his voice. Either that or she had a natural talent for sensing when to plant the hook and when to give more line, because she backed off without a hint of the frustration she must be feeling if she'd hoped to talk money with him tonight.

Assuming it was money.

(Assuming it was talk?)

Instead, as Barbara Jean pressed Lev for more details of my student days in New York, Linville patted her arm gracefully. "If you two are going to monopolize my escort, I shall just go find Chet and make him an offer he cannot refuse."

"That won't be hard," laughed a sturdy brunette who was evidently an old friend of the Winberrys and who had paused on the edge of our conversation. "Come on, honey, let's you and me go jump him while Barbara Jean's got her back turned."

If Linville Pope was half as subtle and deliberate as she appeared to me, I couldn't picture her jumping a man. Even in fun. Nevertheless, she went off with the brunette.

As they melted through the crowd, an ex-assemblyman from Goldsboro who'd once known my mother immediately claimed my attention, and I let myself be swept away by one of those little eddies of movement that swirl through all big parties.

Evidently I still wasn't over my compulsion to put distance between myself and Lev Schuster.

The airy room through which we moved projected in a wing off the main house and had opposing windows and French doors on the two long sides. The furnishings were casually eclectic and reflected their proximity to the water. Seascapes framed in bleached driftwood hung upon the pearl-gray walls, the deep turquoise carpet had probably been woven to order in Burlington, the white wicker chairs and couches were capacious turn-of-the-century originals with modern cushions of blue and seagreen canvas. Shells filled the clear glass bases of the table lamps, and a collection of old iron tools hung above the gray stone fireplace. I recognized an adze and mallet that would have been used in boat building, a saw, C-clamps, brace-and-bit, even an old froe, plus several more I couldn't identify.

At the opposite end, glass shelves held a stunning collection of handmade decoys, everything from a redheaded duck carved from wood to an old swan with a wooden head and painted canvas-and-wire body that should have been in a museum.

("What does stewed swan taste like?" I'd once asked Andy Bynum.

"Well, I personally don't like it as much as stewed loon," he'd answered in all seriousness.)

The elderly assemblyman murmured pleasantly about knowing Mother and my Aunt Zell when they worked at Seymour Johnson Air Field near the end of World War II. He professed himself unable to get over "how very like little Susan Stephenson you are."

Normally I'd have hung on every syllable. My mother died when I was eighteen and though she'd told me most of her secrets, I knew there were things about her Seymour Johnson days that she'd left unsaid. Yet I couldn't concentrate on his words.

"May I come talk to you when we can speak more freely?" I asked above the dull roar of so many conversations going at once.

"Why certainly, my dear. Only don't leave it too long. I'm eighty-three," he warned.

We exchanged cards just as Micah Smith came up with my Bloody Mary, "Lost you there for a few minutes," he said by way of apology for the delay.

"No problem." I sipped my drink gratefully and made for the open French doors on the sea side of the room, only half-attuned to the waves of talk that washed over my ears as I passed.

"—'course my daddy always said a scalloper won't nothing but a fisherman with his brains knocked out."

"—so figuring seventy percent occupancy, that's still more than sixty million dollars right here in Carteret County alone, and if you factor in the motels alone from here to Dare—"

"Yeah, well let the so-called 'private sector' stay private instead of grabbing their profits and passing the real costs downwind and downstream to the public taxpayers."

"The people of this state have an obligation—a *duty*, dammit!—to bring a vision of what this area is to be."

"—but I don't see why the whole of Taylors Creek's got to be a no-wake zone. Why *shouldn't* water-skiers have the right to ski where they want? One of my customers—"

"Oh, they'll *say* a menhaden's the soybean of the ocean, but try asking for the same subsidies those crybaby farmers get and see if—"

"—one thing to stick up for your constituents but for Basnight to bring the legislature into it when—"

"Yeah, but if Marine Fisheries would just use the power they already have—"

I stepped back to let two chamber of commerce types pass (green blazers, plaid pants) and landed myself between a passionate young social scientist and the owner of a tackle shop.

"Commercial fishing's had its day," the tackle man was saying. "Carteret County gets a hundred times more money from tourism than—"

"Only because upstate pollution's killing the estuaries and the recreation industry's driving traditional watermen off the water," the sociologist interrupted. "If you're an uneducated black or white blue-collar worker, your only slice of the tourism pie's going to be cleaning motel rooms or clerking at the local Seven-Eleven for minimum wages. We've got to have better-paying blue-collar jobs if we're ever—"

She paused to snag a glass of white wine from a passing tray, and the tackle shop owner jumped back in. "Look, if they're so almighty anxious to work, how come the crab houses have to hire Mexicans to pick the crabmeat?"

"Don't you reckon that's because Mexicans'll work like slaves under slave-like conditions?" drawled a tall white-haired man who looked like he just stepped off a plantation veranda.

Goes to show you about stereotypes.

I edged past and out onto the terrace, which was less crowded. The air was cooler, but laced with cigarette smoke and something else.

"Uh-oh, the wind's shifting," someone said, as the homely smell of cooking fish drifted lightly across the grounds.

It wasn't an unpleasant aroma, but I had to admit that it did take away something of the bucolic sophistication of Linville Pope's cocktail party.

I hadn't yet seen the Llewellyns, Mr. and Mrs. Docksider; but down by the water, Claire Montgomery sat on the grass like Alice in Wonderland, with her full-skirted blue dress spread out around her. From this distance, it appeared that her hand puppet was also dressed in blue and it seemed to be carrying on a lively conversation with some of the younger male guests.

Across the terrace, raucous laughter centered around the wildlife officer who'd testified in my court this afternoon. I recognized a couple of attorneys and one of the ADAs, but as I began to thread my way over, I was delayed by a man who gave a friendly smile of recognition. "Judge."

"Good evening, Mr.—um—"

"Hudpeth," he reminded me. "Willis Hudpeth. And this is my brother, Telford."

The family likeness was unmistakable. Both men appeared to be late thirties or early forties. Dark brown hair and the tanned faces of outdoorsmen. Rather handsome faces now that I looked twice. (Never hurts to check.)

Telford Hudpeth's handshake was nicely firm as his brother said, "Those bounced checks—the guy from Kinston that bought two rods and then came back the next day and gave me another rubber check for a sixty-dollar reel? Judge Knott here heard the case today and got me a little justice."

Now I remembered. Hudpeth owned a fishing pier over on Atlantic Beach.

"I guess it's hard to remember every case," said Willis Hudpeth.

"No, I remember yours. I gave the defendant a suspended sentence conditional upon his working out a repayment plan with you and paying a fine. You must get a lot of that in season."

"Not as much as you might think. Most sportsmen are pretty honest."

I shook my head. "Practically all I've heard since I got down here is the controversy between recreational and commercial fishermen. I suppose you want to get rid of netters, too."

"Well, no, ma'am, not particularly," he answered, surprising the hell out of me.

"But I thought pier owners—"

"Look," he said patiently. "Drive onto Atlantic Beach and the first pier you come to, Sportsman's Pier, the first thing you see is that big sign, 'You Should Have Been Here Yesterday.' The reason it's there's because fishermen always grumble when they don't catch fish. Maybe they don't have the right rigs, maybe they don't know the first thing about fishing, or maybe the fish just aren't biting that day. You spend a couple of hundred to come down to the coast and you don't catch anything but pinfish, then you can get mad at yourself or mad at the fish or mad at the pier owner. But if the pier owner says, 'Hey, pal, it's them netters out there that's catching all your fish,' who you going to blame?"

"But stop nets do stop fish," I said, enjoying the novelty of his position enough to play devil's advocate.

"Well, of course they do. But if they stopped *all* the fish, crews on the east would be richer'n Midas and those working the westernmost part of Bogue Banks would be poorer'n Job's house cat."

"You're a most unusual pier owner, Mr. Hudpeth. I'm surprised you're here this evening."

"Because I don't agree with Linville Pope's solution to every problem? Know thy enemy's what they preach in my church."

"Is she the enemy?"

"Not Willis's," said Telford Hudpeth. "And not mine either particularly. No, he means *she's* the one wants to know who's thinking what. That's why she invites people from all walks."

"And what's your walk?" I asked him.

"Oh, I'm one of those independent fishermen the other pier owners grumble about."

I'd already picked up on their "hoi toide" accent, yet it wasn't just their measured views that intrigued me. Maybe I was stumbling over stereotypes again, but Telford and Willis Hudpeth in their well-cut jackets, oxford cotton shirts, and tailored slacks seemed a far cry from a Harkers Islander like Mahlon Davis.

"So fishing really can compete with a shore job?"

He nodded. "Beats flipping hamburgers by a fair bit."

His brother laughed. "Buys a brand new car every few years, takes his boys to Europe every summer—yeah, it's a fair bit."

"But how can you make money when so many others complain that sportsmen are running them off the water?"

"I treat it like a business and I fish the whole cycle," he answered matter-of-factly. "I shrimp in the spring, long-haul in summer, sink-net in the fall, scallop in the winter."

Willis Hudpeth nodded approvingly. "Most islanders, they'll wait on a shrimp set and wait and wait till they get the gold mine and maybe they'll bring in two or three hundred pounds. Set out there two or three nights, sometimes longer, and make four or five hundred dollars in just one good night."

"So?"

"So then they won't go back out again for maybe a week or ten days. Not till their money's all gone again. Telford here'll channel-net every night. Maybe only get forty or fifty pounds some nights, but he's averaging a hundred and fifty, two hundred dollars every night, five nights a week during shrimping season. His hours are just as regular as mine. Just as regular as yours maybe."

Telford looked a little embarrassed by his brother's bragging. "Willis works just as hard. Nobody gave him that pier. It's how we were raised. And we're not the only ones living on Harkers Island that have something to show at the end of the year. It's just that Down Easters have always been sort of independent and—"

"Independent?" I snorted. "Bunch of anarchists is what I've heard."

He smiled. "Well, it's true we don't like anybody telling us what to do—not a boss man, not the government, and sometimes not even our own good sense. That's mainly why a lot of Islanders won't work as regularly as they could. They say they'd as soon punch a time clock over to Cherry Point if they can't fish when they want to and lay out when they don't want to."

Some people nearby vacated a set of white canvas lawn chairs and we claimed them. The ice was starting to melt in my Bloody Mary, but I was too interested in this different view of the water to go looking for a fresh drink. Besides, their words had triggered Mahlon's.

"Where do you sell your catch?"

"Might be any one of several places," Telford Hudpeth said. "Whoever's giving top dollar."

"Bynum's?"

"That's right," Willis remembered. "You were the first out to Andy, weren't you? Wonder if they'll ever catch who did it?"

"Why would a fisherman call him the man?"

"Depends on who he is," said Telford. "Everybody that runs a fish house gets called that at one time or another. See, a fish house can't survive if it doesn't have people out there fishing for it, so some of 'em might weight the nets a little in their favor—stake a man to new nets, give him gas on credit, maybe even help him buy a boat and let him fish on shares."

Willis Hudpeth agreed. "'I'll just take ten percent till you work out the boat,' he'll say."

"Only you've got to sell your ninety percent to him at his price," said Telford Hudpeth.

"And his price is lower than what other fish houses might be paying?"

"Some people owe the man all their lives," Telford answered soberly. "I don't want to live like that myself."

Micah Smith paused with a tray of hot crab puffs and we all three took a couple. "May I get you another one of those, Judge?" he asked, pointing to my glass.

I shook my head. "But I sure could use a big glass of ice water."

"Coming right up. Gentlemen?"

Both indicated that they would nurse the drinks they had.

I bit into the luscious morsel of creamy crabmeat and delicate crust.

"One thing my brother didn't mention," said Telford as he downed his crab puff in one mouthful, "is if the man's a flat-out cheat and his scales are off. In his favor, of course. Because half the time you don't know what you've made till he pulls up on Saturday morning with your money. He tells you what your catch weighed out to. What you get depends on the price the wholesaler pays *him* and some weeks there's such a glut of fish you don't even make your gas money back if you're working for the man."

"Was Andy Bynum dishonest?"

Willis looked uncertain, but Telford shook his head. "Never did wrong by me that I know of, but I didn't *have* to sell my fish to him, see? A lot of people did." He paused and added cryptically, "And a lot of people always think it's the man's fault when things don't shake out the way they think it ought to."

"You must be a member of the Alliance."

"Yes, ma'am. I don't know how much seiners have in common with tongers, but *all* watermen are under pressure, no matter what Willis says. That's where we're going to really miss Andy. He could near 'bout talk a hermit crab right out of its conch shell."

Micah Smith returned with a large goblet of water and Telford passed it over to me with a troubled look in his clear blue eyes. "You asked me if

Andy was dishonest. Not with money, maybe, and not by cheating with his scales, but I have to say that if he knew he might help the Alliance by twisting something around, I believe he'd do it, don't you, Will?"

Willis Telford's answer was lost beneath the sudden blast of a shotgun. I jumped up, heard a woman cry, "Pull!" then another crack of the gun and a clay pigeon exploded in midair over the water.

Unnoticed by the three of us, most of the party had drifted out to the landing.

"Trapshooting?" I've hunted quail and rabbits with my brothers, but I'd never done any fancy shooting.

"Part of the entertainment," said Telford Hudpeth. "She's got a bunch of guns and most people like to shoot, but this is usually where we cut out. Besides, we wait any longer, I'm going to miss the tide." He held out his hand. "Been a pleasure, ma'am. You're staying down the island in that little yellow house next to Mahlon Davis, right?"

I nodded, unsurprised that he should know. Fishermen and farmers have a lot in common.

"Maybe I'll drop you off some fresh shrimp," he said.

I walked with them as far as the landing so that I could watch the trapshooters who stood on the dock and shot out over the marshes beyond.

There were a couple of men and two women, each with shotguns that our hostess seemed to have provided. One of the women was Barbara Jean and she called, "Come on, Deborah, let's see how good your eye is."

I made weak protests. Truth is, it looked like fun and she only had to urge me twice to take her place.

Even a twenty-gauge can give a nice little kick, but I was used to a sixteen so it didn't bother me. This was a simple contest. Several yards downshore and out of the line of fire, one of the men operated a small mechanical trap thrower, and the four of us fired in rotation till we missed.

I know it's not politically correct to enjoy shooting, and given the option I'd certainly vote for much stricter gun control; but we all know it's not a constitutional issue no matter what the NRA says. Why else would so many men use gun images to describe sex?

"Hotter'n a two-dollar pistol."

"Shot my wad."

"Firing blanks."

All that power, all that force and all you have to do is pull a trigger.

To my delight, I hit my first ceramic disk square in the middle. And my second. In fact, I didn't get put out till the fourth round. It helped my ego that two of the other three missed their fourth rounds, too.

As I surrendered my gun and was heading for the house for another glass of water, I heard Lev's taunting voice behind me. "Shotguns? You went totally native, didn't you, Red?"

"Absolutely." I turned and let my eyes rake the length of his body, from his expensively barbered head to his Italian shoes. "Haven't you?"

His smile faded. "Touché."

"I didn't even recognize you in court today," I said accusingly. "And it wasn't just the beard either."

"I recognized you."

Despite the blasting guns, an uneasy silence stretched between us as we each examined the other for changes. There were flecks of gray in his dark hair, more gray in a beard that was new to me, lines around those intense deep-set eyes that hadn't been there when we lived together, an unfamiliar attention to clothes.

And what was he seeing?

My hair—light brown or dark blonde depending on the season—was shorter these days, I was probably five pounds heavier, and my face showed similar signs of the passing years, though I now disguised the lines with makeup I once scorned as completely as he'd scorned name-brand labels.

Then he gave me that funny little scrunch of a shrug and all at once, he was just Lev again.

"Truce?" he said.

"Truce." Almost against my will, I felt my lips curve in a smile of pure pleasure. "How *are* you, Lev? And what are you doing in Beaufort with that weird Montgomery gal?"

"Pleasure, mostly. Some business. And Claire's not really weird."

"Somebody who can only talk through a hand puppet?" A thought crossed my mind. "You're not married to her, are you?"

He laughed. "God, no! No, she's my partner's sister. They were in court today, too."

"I saw them," I reminded him dryly. "I also saw that disgustingly vulgar boat. *Rainmaker?* Yours or Llewellyn's?"

He looked embarrassed. "Ours. It was in lieu of some fees actually."

I remembered now that he hadn't answered my earlier question. I rephrased it. "What sort of practice are you in that you get boats like that for fees?"

A burst of laughter from the crowd drowned out his answer.

"What?"

"We handle divorces."

"You're kidding. That's your whole practice?"

Okay, we've all gotten older, more cynical, more interested in security maybe, less interested in ethics, but to sell out so completely? "Somehow I never pictured you as part of the *Me-Me-Me* decade."

Again that quirky shrug. "I thought we had a truce."

"Sorry."

"The paper said you found a body Sunday night?"

"Yes." I didn't want to discuss it; didn't want Andy Bynum's death and the way I'd found him to be part of idle cocktail chatter.

As if he could still read my mind, Lev changed the subject yet again. "Your friend also tells me you've been a judge almost a year?"

"Since last June, yes."

"You like the view better from that side of the bench?" Another round of shooting began and Lev flinched with distaste. "I've heard that every damn pickup in the south has a gun rack in the back, but I didn't know women got off on guns, too."

Anyone else I'd have accused of chauvinism. In Lev's case, I figured it must be the alien corn he was standing in.

We had a good view from where we stood and the shooters now were two Jaycee types, Barbara Jean and Linville Pope. After another four rounds, only the two women were still in. Chet said they'd had four guns stolen and now I realized at least one of them must have been Barbara Jean's. Linville barely came up to Barbara Jean's shoulder, but her barrel followed the arc of the clay pigeon just as smoothly as she shattered her fifth in a row.

It was so incongruous. Barbara Jean in pearls, heels and a slinky dress, the late afternoon sunlight turning her blonde curls strawberry as she killed her sixth "bird" in a row; Linville in a floral silk cocktail suit, carefully tucking her hair behind her ears and out of her eyes before she loaded and fired a sixth time.

As the eighth round began, Barbara Jean missed. "Pull," said Linville and, without glancing at the ceramic disc, shot her gun straight up into the air.

The crowd clapped her show of good sportsmanship and Barbara Jean shook her head, but her smile was just a little too bright as she handed her gun over to Chet, who had stepped up for the next round of competition.

With the shooting making coherent conversation almost impossible, we stepped back inside the house and made for the bar. Both barmen were down helping with the guns, so Lev poured himself a whiskey and soda and I refilled my glass of ice water, then we passed through the opposite set of French doors onto a narrower terrace completely walled on all three sides with head-high azaleas that dazzled the eye with clear pinks and corals, vibrant reds and cool whites.

Muffled gunshots and massed azaleas.

Lev shook his head and chanted, "And that's what I like about the South!"

As our eyes met, we heard the clink of glassware, then voices in the room behind us.

"I don't need any fucking concessions from you," a woman said angrily. I recognized Barbara Jean's voice.

"No? But you will take them from everyone else?" came Linville Pope's quiet silky tones.

A questioning sound.

"The way you play the beleaguered benefactor to twenty-three black families—that *is* how you put it every time anybody tries to regulate your trawlers? Twenty-three black families who could not buy even a gallon of milk if not for the paychecks you sign? So easy to play the race card when it suits you, but I have done a little research on Neville Fishery. What happened to all the black families that were cut loose when your father switched over to hydraulic winches to pull the nets and started using hoses to suction the fish out of those nets?"

"You leave my daddy out of this."

"Look, Barbara Jean—" Her voice was that of a patient adult reasoning with a fractious child. "The tide is running out. Fishing was a wonderful way of life. *Last* century. Menhaden generate what? Four million a year? Tourism brings in half a billion. Face it, honey, you are history. Maybe not this year, maybe not next, but it is coming. That little factory of yours sits squat in the middle of—"

"I'd die before I'd sell it to you," Barbara Jean snarled.

"No one is asking you to," Linville soothed. "My principals are the ones who want it bad enough to offer you more than it is worth."

"My granddaddy built that factory and my grandsons—"

I missed the rest because Lev put his lips close to my ear and whispered, "There has to be a path somewhere through those flower bushes. Maybe there at that corner?"

I hesitated.

(*"Knowledge is power,"* the pragmatist reminded me, straining to hear what was being said just inside those open doors.)

(*"And you were accusing HIM of lapsed standards?"* the preacher lectured.)

Reluctantly, I tiptoed after Lev, across the terrace and through the bushes.

Eventually we broke through that floral barrier to a green lawn of billiard table perfection.

"Have dinner with me?" asked Lev.

"You mean just leave quietly without telling anybody and go find a place where the only discussion of fish is whether to have it grilled or fried? You got it!"

We crossed the grass to the circular paved drive where eight or ten shiny cars were parked.

"Which one's yours?" he asked.

I might have known it wasn't going to be that simple.

Lev quirked his eyebrows at me as I stood laughing beneath a live oak tattered with Spanish moss. "What's so funny?"

"I came by boat. You, too?"

He nodded. "With Catherine, Jon and Claire."

"I came with Barbara Jean and Chet Winberry," I said.

"Don't tell me. Barbara Jean's the one having that, um, discussion with our hostess?"

"'Fraid so."

"Hm-mm-m."

⌘

It took us a few minutes to work our way through the front hall and out onto the seaward terrace without going near the sunroom wing. Somehow I doubted that Linville Pope would notice if I didn't go thank her for inviting me. I spotted Barbara Jean heading for the dock and hurried after her with only a "See you" flung over my shoulder for Lev.

Out on the driveway, we had decided that if we could prod our respective ferrymen into leaving early, we would each return the way we'd come, then meet at one of the restaurants off Front Street as soon as we could politely disentangle ourselves.

Judging by Barbara Jean's purposeful stride, I wasn't going to have to do much prodding. I saw her speak to Chet, who put his arm around her, then looked back toward the house for me. I waved that I was coming and soon joined them at their mooring.

Barbara Jean was so furious she was almost crying with barely controlled rage. "That bitch!" she kept saying. "That bitch. That absolute *bitch!*"

Chet made placating noises and threw me an apologetic glance as he cast off.

"Something wrong?" I leaned my forearms on the back of their seat and gazed from one profile to the other.

"That—that—"

"Bitch?" I offered helpfully.

Chet laughed and even Barbara Jean gave a rueful smile.

"Yeah," she said.

She twisted around in her seat so that she faced both of us and said, "First she said my factory's history and now she's trying to blackmail me into selling it to her."

"What?" said Chet.

"Blackmail?" I said. "That's a pretty strong term."

She gave an impatient flip of her hand. "Not blackmail. What's the term? Coercion? That's what she's trying to do, coerce me."

"But how?" Chet and I asked together.

"Jill," she said, and her anger abruptly dissolved into tears that spilled down her cheeks.

"Honey?"

"Oh Chet, she's bought Gib Epson's place!" she wailed. "She says she's already got the permits and that I have till the first of June to decide, then she's going to start building a launch ramp and boat storage for a hundred boats. There'll be cars in and out, day and night, all year long!"

Chet hit the wheel with his fist. "But Epson swore he'd never sell."

"She made him a fat offer and let him think it was a conservancy group that wanted it. He probably thinks he was doing us a favor." She reached into Cher's pocket for his handkerchief and blotted her eyes in pensive silence.

We were moving a little faster around the point than when we'd come. The wind ruffled our hair and felt cool enough to make me wish for a sweater now that the sun was dropping down behind the trees.

"How does your daughter come into it?" I asked.

"My mother was from Harkers Island," Barbara Jean explained, "and she inherited the home place over there. The original part of the house dates from the 1890s. She really loved it and she always wanted to go live there, but Daddy had the factory over here and what with one thing or another, they never got to restore the house the way she wanted. She used to take Jill over and tell her all the old family stories and Jill was wild about it, too, so when Mother died, she willed it to Jill and she and her husband have put every nickel they have into fixing it up. They've just finished."

More tears pooled in her eyes and she dashed them away angrily. "And now that bitch—!"

"I take it that the bitch's new property abuts yours?"

"Even curves around one side," Chet said grimly.

"But surely your zoning laws—?"

Chet shook his head. "Harkers Island is like the rest of Down East. They're so adamantly opposed to any kind of growth or government interference that they won't allow any zoning of any kind."

"That's crazy," I said. "Zoning's the only way a community can control growth and have a say in what's built."

"Well, why don't you just run on over and tell them that if you get a few minutes off from court?" Chet said with asperity. "You think people haven't tried? Every time the county planners try to hold a hearing on the subject and explain how zoning would protect them, they're lucky to get away with their lives."

"Down Easters don't think they need zoning," Barbara Jean said as Chet throttled back on the motor and headed in toward their landing. "My cousin over in Marshallburg said that if somebody ever tried to build something the rest of them didn't want, they'd just burn it down. They would, too."

"Maybe we'll sic your cousin on to Linville's boat storage," Chet said.

"Hey!" I objected. "I'm an officer of the court and I didn't hear a thing you just said, okay?"

Chet nosed us in next to the dock and secured a line to the piling. I scrambled out and Chet reached out a hand to Barbara Jean, who hadn't moved. "Honey?"

She took his hand and stood up slowly. "All of a sudden, I remember something Andy said."

"Andy Bynum?"

"Remember how he was rooting around in the courthouse all this month? And last week at the Alliance meeting—you remember when you came to pick me up and I was standing out front with Andy and Jay Hadley and her son?"

Chet nodded.

"You must have heard him. Andy said he'd found something that was going to fix Linville Pope's little red wagon once and for all and—oh my God!

She clutched Cher's arm hard. "What if Andy really did find some-thing illegal? What if he threatened to tell if she didn't back off? She's got a boat, she's got a gun and she's got the conscience of a sand shark—maybe she's the one who shot him out there in the sound."

CHAPTER 7

Launch out into the deep,
Oh, let the shoreline go;
Launch out, launch out in the ocean divine,
Out where the full tides go.

But many, alas! only stand on the shore
And gaze on the ocean so wide;
They never have ventured its depths to explore,
Or to launch on the fathomless tide.

—A. B. Simpson and B. B. McKinney

"Now let me get this straight," said Lev. "This Andy Bynum was a fisherman, right?"

"A fisherman, the owner of a fish house and the president of the Independent Fishers Alliance," I said, nibbling at a shrimp from my Mate's Plate (cole slaw, hushpuppies and three seafood choices from a list of eight; the Captain's Plate lets you choose four; the Admiral's, five).

"And your friend Barbara Ann—"

"Barbara Jean."

"Whatever. Her husband's a judge and she owns a fishmeal plant, right?"

"Right."

"So how do fishing interests conflict with Pope Properties?"

We were sitting in a candlelit booth at the Long Haul, one block off Front Street, but for a moment it was like being back in that old fourth-floor walk-up on the Upper West Side in Manhattan, sharing Chinese takeout while Lev helped me clarify the facts of a case for next day's class.

He lifted his empty beer bottle when the waitress passed and she nodded. "Another for you, ma'am?"

My glass of house "blush" was still half full, so I shook my head and went back to explaining a situation I didn't fully comprehend myself even though I'd asked a lot of questions and listened to a lot of polemics the short time I'd been down.

"The way I understand it, there are four major interests pulling at the coastal waters here in North Carolina: environmentalists; commercial fishing—that's workers on and off the water; recreational fishing—motels, piers, marinas, boat sales, tackle shops, and all the other tourist-support businesses; and finally the developers who seem to want managed growth as long as it's everybody else who's being managed."

"So what else is new?" Lev asked sardonically.

"Trouble is, it doesn't stay that simple. Depending on what's being discussed, alliances seem to switch back and forth with the tides. Environmentalists will ally with either or both groups of fishermen against the developers. Fishermen ally with them because they've seen what pollution does to the estuaries and they've already lost too many shellfish beds. Now the conservationist wing—"

"Aren't they the same as environmentalists?"

"I don't think so. Not exactly. At least not the way they define it down here. Conservationists want to save the water, too, but their main interest seems to be endangered species, especially turtles. They give the trawlers grief because nets have to use excluder devices to let the turtles escape. Or the size of the net mesh has to be big enough to let certain species through, stuff like that. And they irk sportsmen because they're always pushing size and catch limits and they'd like to keep all recreational vehicles off the beach during nesting season. Come to think of it, the fishermen hate the turtle excluders, but they line up beside the conservationists to keep surf fishers from making such deep wheel ruts on the sand that baby turtles can't get back to the sea in time."

Lev laughed. "Do they really care, or is it tit for tat?"

"Well, if sportsmen would support getting rid of the TEDs, the fishermen probably wouldn't be stressing themselves overmuch on baby turkles."

"Turkles?"

"That's what Islanders say when they talk about turkle stew," I said, thinking of the loggerhead shell I'd seen rolling in the surf by Mahlon's landing the night before.

"Wait a minute. You just said they're an endangered species."

"They are. Just like loons. But they're also a traditional island delicacy, which is why they both keep getting their heads blown off."

He rolled his eyes in amusement. "Go on."

"It gets worse. I swear to God every interest group down here's shooting at loons of one sort or the other—each one thinks that what they're doing doesn't *really* hurt anything and it's the other guys that are messing it up for everybody else. Fish processors ally with developers against environmentalists because they don't want anybody looking too closely at their waste disposal procedures. But then the developers turn around and talk environment whenever they can because they know if our coastline starts looking like New Jersey's, the Crystal Coast is a cooked goose. No more golden eggs."

"I still don't see why poor Linville's supposed to have it in for a fisherman," he complained.

"I'm getting to that. Have another hushpuppy and listen," I said testily, wondering what was this *poor Linville* crap? "She's allied herself with the sports fishers against the menhaden boats."

He finished boning his grilled mackerel and said, "What the hell is a menhaden anyhow? I've never seen it on a menu."

"That's because you're not a chicken. After the oil is pressed out, the leftover meal is used for feed and fertilizer."

"That's what Barbara What's-her-name's factory processes?"

"Right. But the whole controversy's turning into a class thing—traditional livelihoods up against privileged leisure.

"See, what you have to keep in mind is that this place didn't start booming and become the Crystal Coast till the late seventies, early eighties," I said. "Down Easters lived so isolated and insular that they just assumed God gave them Core Sound back when He first laid down the waters and He meant it for their personal use till the last trumpet sounds. Then down come these upstate sportsmen who can afford to drop three or four hundred for a weekend of fishing. They're after the same fish a working man's trying to catch to feed his family and maybe make a mortgage and boat payments. So you start with that resentment between natives and visitors."

"But if menhaden aren't edible," Lev said, keeping his eye on the shifting target, "then why—?"

"According to Barbara Jean, menhaden fishing's gotten a bad rap both from the sportsmen and from some of the rich retirees along the coast who don't want to look out from their decks and see big old rusty boats sitting out there off their beach. The stock is healthy, they're not overfished, and they're easy to catch because they run in tight schools close to the shoreline. And that's where the trouble seems to be. About seventy-five percent of the catch is within a quarter mile of the shore. So here comes Barbara Jean's clunky old *Washington Neville*. Or Beaufort Fisheries' *Gregory Poole*. The big boat sends out two little purse boats to surround the school of fish with a long net that they can draw up tight at the bottom like a purse. Then the mother boat sucks the fish up with a big hose. People on shore are close enough to see exactly what's happening and they think 'O, my Gawd! Look at that ugly greedy ship taking all those fish!' And the sportsman who's out there casting in the surf and not getting any good bites thinks, 'They've just scooped up all the game fish.'"

"And haven't they?" asked Lev, pouring himself a fresh glass of beer.

"Local watermen joke that anybody who can catch a menhaden on a hook is welcome to try and no, the bycatch of game fish is incredibly small—something like three-tenths of one percent because there's nothing in that school *except* menhaden."

"But if a net broke—"

"I'm told there hasn't been a spill worth talking about since 1983 and that was up in Virginia."

"But why—?"

"I know, I know. Why poor Linville?"

"Well?"

"Because she's been a very vocal supporter for limits on how close in the menhaden boats can come. She's even gone up to Raleigh to lobby some of the legislators and they say she's very persuasive. When people like Barbara Jean or Andy Bynum start yelling in these hearings, she just hangs cool and manages to sound calm and objective and beautifully reasonable. If the boats do get pushed out of the sound and two or three miles offshore, it'll hurt the industry enough that it may not survive. But Andy thought, and Barbara Jean does, too, that menhaden's just the stalking horse, a foot in the door."

"For what?"

"Well, from listening to everybody mouth off about everybody else, there probably is too much equipment in the water down here. Especially since the estuaries are getting so much polluted runoff that nursery stocks can't replenish what's being taken out. If they could get rid of all the commercial fishers, then it'd really be a sportsman's paradise. You heard Linville this evening—right now, tourism's worth half a billion to this area and growing, menhaden's only worth about four million and dropping. But from what she said to Barbara Jean, I think it's more than just gentrifying Carteret County. She wants that particular piece of property where the Neville Fishery sits, doesn't she? Is that part of the investment deal she's trying to get you to buy into?"

Lev looked thoughtful. "As you say, she's very persuasive. I did think things were a little further along."

"Like claiming title to property she doesn't have?"

"Oh no. She's too sharp for that." He gave me a quizzical look. "You still haven't learned to play chess yet, have you?"

"I remember the moves," I lied.

"Well, Linville Pope has the makings of a natural chess player—always looking eight moves ahead. She sees the ramifications, knows that what happens on this move makes what happens later absolutely inevitable. I'm going to have to watch her closer than I realized. Interesting lady."

That I would never take chess seriously was one of the things that had rasped him. He loved the game's complexity and admired deviousness in his opponents.

I personally think that bridge and poker call for just as much deviousness. Of course, they also call for more than two players. Was that a fundamental difference?

"So how interesting would you say she is?" I asked, pushing my plate aside. "Would she kill?"

"Not for any reason you've laid out here. The woman's bright, beautiful and seems to work hard *and* smart. Maybe she's a little too cute about the way she acquires property, but what she's offering your friend sounds like a good deal to me. I've looked that factory over from the outside and even if the fishing continues, it's probably going to need a lot of capital repairs. I bet her whole operation wouldn't bring a half-million, if that, on today's market."

How casually he tossed off half a million dollars. I was suddenly remembering the tons of pasta we ate because his fellowship money always ran out before the month did.

"Do you still have that book—*A Hundred Ways With Pasta?*"

"Is that another dig about my current living standards?"

"Not to mention current moral standards if you don't see anything wrong with coercing someone to sell."

He went into his Daniel Webster mode. "You don't think your friend might have exaggerated?"

"Barbara Jean *can* go off half-cocked," I conceded. "But not without something to light her fuse. She certainly didn't dream up that thing about a boat ramp and storage next door to her ancestral home."

"But accusing Linville of murdering a fisherman sounds like wishful thinking to me."

First it was poor Linville and then it was Linville the bright and beautiful. "Just how long have you known this woman anyhow?" I asked nastily.

"Long enough to know she wouldn't do something that vicious or stupid."

"Coffee?" chirped our waitress.

I nodded; Lev said, "Cappuccino?"

"Sorry, sir."

"Espresso, then."

"I'm sorry sir, we just have regular and decaf."

"Decaf then," he said ungraciously; and when she'd brought it, he grumbled, "If this town hopes to keep tourists coming back, it's going to have to get serious about its coffee."

"If the whole world turns into Manhattan, how will you know when you're on vacation?" I asked sweetly.

In a familiar gesture of exasperation, he ran his hand through his hair and wiry tufts stood up angrily. Some things even a fifty-dollar haircut can't change.

He saw my amusement, started to bristle and then suddenly smiled. "Why the hell are we talking about Linville Pope and Barbara Jean What's-her-name and fishmeal factories when we should be talking about us? You know, I pictured a thousand times running into you again. I never expected to find you sitting on the bench in a little town on the Intracoastal Waterway."

I was willing to play and smiled back at him over my coffee cup. "How *did* you imagine it?"

"That we were both back in New York on a visit and we bumped into each other over the cheese counter at Zabar's or standing in line for *Cats* or—"

"Only in Manhattan?" I teased gently.

"Nothing brought me down to Raleigh and I couldn't picture you in Boston. Were you?"

I shook my head.

"What about the Clara Barton Rest Stop on the Jersey Turnpike seven years ago near the end of August?"

His big hands toyed with the glass candleholder as he tried to make his tone light.

"Were you really there?" I asked, incredulous. "Why on earth didn't you speak to me?"

He shrugged. "You were with some other women."

"Three of my brothers' wives," I remembered. "We probably *were* on our way to see *Cats.*"

"I had just pulled in and you passed right in front of my car. You had on white shorts and a red shirt and your hair was still long."

"I'm sorry," I whispered.

"Ah, what the hell?" He pushed the candle away and signaled for the bill. "Let's walk."

⌘

It always amazes me what walkers city people are. We've got the wide open spaces and farm work requires a certain amount of walking, but nothing like city life. Probably because we don't categorize feet as a genuine form of transportation. When there are fences to mend down by the creek or if you need to take a jug of water to someone plowing new ground out behind the pasture, you jump in a pickup with four-wheel drive. City people—especially New Yorkers—think nothing of walking two country miles to go pick up a library book.

"Can't we take a bus?" I used to whine, cabs being out of our price range.

"But it's only thirty blocks," Lev would say heartlessly.

Yet when we weren't rushing to get somewhere before the doors closed or the lights went down, walking in the city could be wonderful. Beaufort was no city, of course, but we walked through the cool night air and enjoyed the old white clapboard houses, the antique store windows, the deserted sidewalks back up from the water. Tourist season was only beginning so we mostly had those side streets to ourselves even though it wasn't yet ten o'clock.

By tacit consent, our talk was of life in Boston, life in Colleton County, how I'd come to the bench, where are they now all the people we'd known, and who do you suppose lived in this great white house with the widow's walk?

Eventually we wound up near the Ritchie House, the only place still open and still serving drinks. But as he started to open the glass door to the lounge, Lev said, "Oh hell!" and stepped back quickly.

Through the glass I saw the Docksiders seated at one of the lounge tables with a couple of attorneys I recognized from court. Mrs. Llewellyn's hair was a swirl of dandelion gold as she threw back her head and laughed at something one of the men had said. There was no sign of Claire Montgomery.

"You're not in the mood for more cocktail chatter, are you?" Lev asked.

"Not really." And certainly not with people I'd effectively ruled against in court.

We walked back along the boardwalk where all the boats were moored. A northeast breeze whipped my hair, and low music from someone's radio mingled with the sound of lapping water. A few of the decks had people sitting outside enjoying the quiet night, but most had gone below, with only a dim glow showing behind curtained windows.

Beneath one of the security lights, I paused and checked my watch. Nearly eleven.

Lev suddenly took my hand and said, "Don't go yet. Let's have our nightcap on the *Rainmaker.*"

"Better give me a raincheck," I demurred. "I'm not up to small talk with a puppet."

"Oh Claire won't be there. When we're in port, they wimp out and stay ashore. Their baby—well, actually Nicky's not really a baby any more—but it's still easier to manage him in a hotel. It was a fluke that Claire was even here the day that bike was taken. No, they have a suite at the Ritchie House. Linville's a friend of the owners."

No doubt. Barbara Jean said that handling the Ritchie House had been her first big coup a few years back.

"No strings," he promised as I hesitated.

(*"Not a good idea,"* said the preacher.)

(*"The books are closed on this,"* agreed the pragmatist. *"You sure you want to open them again?"*)

I ignored both warnings and followed Lev down the pier to the *Rainmaker's* slip. I told myself it was only because I'd never been below

93

on a private boat this size before. It would be interesting to see the fittings.

("*Yeah, we know what fittings you're interested in,*" leered the pragmatist.)

Well, and so what? I argued back. We had been good together once upon a time, and like that old Ray Price song says, what was wrong with one more time for all the good times?

⌘

Except that it trailed a small dinghy instead of a Ford and sported a keel instead of wheels, the outside of the *Rainmaker* was really not much more than a fancier version of the RV that my Aunt Sister and Uncle Rufus drive back and forth to Florida. That resemblance was the real reason I'd even noticed it in the first place. That and the name, of course, which suggested a corporate attorney.

Inside, the similarities were even more pronounced. The interior was bigger than Aunt Sister's Winnebago—she could only sleep four, the *Rainmaker* six, Lev told me—but if it weren't for the gentle motion, you'd be hard pressed to tell much difference. Every inch used, no wasted space, yet it didn't seem cramped because the main cabin felt like a small lounge. The recessed wall lights were dimmed way down. A wide upholstered bench became a sofa berth when the table was flipped back out of the way, and cushions softened the angles.

I slipped one of those cushions under my head and watched lazily as Lev pulled ice cubes from the tiny refrigerator and glasses from a shallow cupboard.

"Still bourbon and—was it Coke?" he asked.

"Pepsi, but Coke's fine. Easy on the bourbon."

The preacher approved, but the pragmatist wasn't fooled. He knew I still hadn't decided whether or not I'd be driving later.

Lev brought our drinks over and sat down beside me. He touched his glass to mine and his dark eyes were unreadable in the soft light.

"To all the good times," he said, echoing my own memories.

I probably took two good sips before carefully setting my glass down where it wouldn't get knocked over.

"I think I like the beard," I said and leaned forward until our lips met—gently, tentatively at first, then with such deepening hunger that searing jets of purely carnal desire shot through me, blocking out all voices of reason and prudence, leaving me sensate and reckless.

His hands. His big and wonderfully familiar hands were everywhere, burning through the thin cream-colored silk of my jumpsuit, touching me where no one else had touched in much too long. I tugged at his shirt, wildly impatient to feel and taste his skin again. His hair tangled in the crystal beads against my breasts. I was trying to untangle them and he was undoing my buttons, when we heard the hatch opening up above.

A light voice called, "Ahoy, the *Rainmaker!*" and slender legs descended the laddered stair. There was a bottle of champagne in one hand, a large purse in the other.

"Did you think I got lost, honey?" Linville Pope caroled. "One of those long-winded—"

She reached the bottom step and the smile on her lips froze as she saw us.

"Oh," she said finally when it seemed as if the leaden silence would go on forever. "You started without me."

Give her points for poise.

Lev had sat up so abruptly that my necklace broke and a shower of crystal spilled into my lap.

"I thought you said you weren't coming," Lev said harshly.

"I said I might not be able to get away," she corrected him quietly. "Obviously I should have called first. Sorry."

Clutching her purse to her chest, a just-in-case purse that probably held a toothbrush and a couple of other necessities should champagne turn into a sleepover, she set the bottle on a nearby counter and turned to go.

"Don't leave on my account." I had rebuttoned my blouse and was now scooping up crystal beads and shoving them into my Mexican purse. "I'm just going myself."

"No," she protested.

"Yes," I said firmly. Passion was gone and so was I, just as soon as I could find my missing shoe. A cold thick rage consumed me.

Lev took one look at my face and silently handed over the high-heeled slipper that had come off before. So at least he'd learned that much over the years.

More beads sparkled across the floor when I stood, but I was too angry to stop. All I wanted was out of there. Linville stood aside to let me pass, but then I heard her steps behind me as she followed me up the ladder and off the boat.

We walked half the length of the planked dock in stony silence until the whole farcical ridiculousness of the situation abruptly hit me and I started giggling.

After a startled glance, Linville Pope gave an unladylike gurgle and by the time we reached the parking area we were both laughing so hard we had to hold onto each other to stand up.

"God! What bastards they can be," she said at last when we had finally gained control again. "Come on over to the Ritchie House and let me get us another bottle of champagne."

"I'm sorely tempted," I told her truthfully, "but I probably shouldn't show up in court tomorrow with a champagne hangover."

⌘

On the long drive back to Harkers Island, though, I almost wished I'd accepted Linville's invitation. I still didn't have a handle on her, but I was starting to like the cut of her jib.

Lots of people came to her party, but Barbara Jean thought she was manipulative and coercive. Chet seemed to find her amusing except when she threatened Barbara Jean's equanimity. Even Lev, damn him to holy hell, thought she was beautiful and smart but "maybe just a little too cute about the way she acquired property." There had been that angry scene in the Ritchie House, something about the fraudulent sale of a boat? And I had a feeling that Mahlon Davis's "bitch over to Beaufort" was going to turn out to be Linville Pope, too.

But anybody who could see the absurdity of the situation tonight and laugh that hard surely couldn't be all bad.

It was well past midnight when I drove up to the cottage. Except for scattered security lights on tall utility poles, all the nearby houses were dark. No light out at Mahlon's, but I saw the shape of Mickey Mantle's pickup parked behind the boat shelter and wondered if his triumph in court had him driving without a license again.

The only thing I could hear was wind in the live oaks and low waves splashing against the shore. I got out of the car, walked up onto the porch, unlocked the door and set my garment bag inside without switching on a light. At that moment, the telephone began to ring—an intrusively mechanical, almost alien sound amid the island's natural quiet. When I picked up the receiver, Lev's voice said, "Red, I—"

I broke the connection, then laid the receiver under the pillow and walked away from its insistent beeping.

The wind was blowing in smartly off the water and it was chilly, but I slipped on Sue's old windbreaker again and went back out to one of the porch rockers, hoping the rhythmic flash of the lighthouse and the sound of the surf would lull me into drowsiness. Seeing Lev again after all these years had roiled up so many old memories and conflicting emotions that if I tried to go sensibly to bed, I knew I'd only toss and turn till morning.

When we met, I was still running from a really stupid marriage, living on part-time jobs and money Aunt Zell sent. It was a bitter cold winter and the New York Public Library was a good place to stay warm. For some reason, I'd gotten it into my head that I needed to read Proust, and that winter, I did. From *Swann's Way* straight through *The Past Recaptured*, though to this day I couldn't describe a single scene or say what those seven books added up to. Yet while I read, I was totally addicted and it seemed to ease my homesickness.

And then one day I lifted up my head and there was Lev across the wide musty room and I realized that he'd been there all winter, too, in the late afternoon, in almost the same chair. Wiry hair in a perpetual tousle, close-knit frame, dark eyes set so far under the ridge of his brow that they were like two secretive intelligent creatures peering out of a cave.

He hadn't noticed me, but once I'd focused on him, I couldn't seem to quit. I circled to see what he was reading. Two of my cousins back in

Dobbs were lawyers and I recognized that those were law books and landmark cases and that he was probably a law student somewhere in the city.

No ring on his finger and no study dates that winter.

Oh what the hell, I thought. I left Proust lying on the table and followed Lev out of the library that evening and when we were almost to the bottom step, I let myself fall against him so that we both went down in a tangle of books and scarves and laughing apology.

I must have slipped on the ice, I told him, and no, nothing seemed broken, but it wouldn't be, would it, not with all the heavy coats and gloves y'all wear up here? He heard my accent (how could he not, the way I was laying it on?) and asked how long I'd been in New York and all I could think was that I'd never seen eyes so dark and piercing and the smell of his aftershave—I could almost smell it now, could almost—

I stopped rocking abruptly.

It wasn't Lev's aftershave I smelled, but a fragrance sweetish and equally well known. I stood up, sniffing now, quartering the wind like one of my daddy's hounds.

Nothing.

Yet, seated in the rocking chair, I smelled it again, an elusively familiar aroma.

Insect repellent?

I walked over to the near end of the porch. In the dim light, did the grass there look scuffed? If I hadn't been looking straight down at it—a dark shape that I'd thought was a rock or a piece of scrap wood—I might not have noticed when it drew back very, very slowly and disappeared under the edge of the porch.

A booted foot.

I sat back down in the rocker and thought about that foot a minute and then went out to the trunk of my car and got the loaded .38 Daddy gave me a few years back when I made it clear I wasn't going to quit driving alone at night or stop looking for witnesses in rough places.

Back up on the porch, I rocked for another couple of minutes, then slid the safety off and said in a low conversational tone, "I don't know why you're under my porch, but if you don't come out now, I'm going to start shooting right through these planks."

I heard a muffled "Oh shit!" and scraping sounds, then a man hauled himself out feet first. As he reached for his pocket, I said, "Keep your hands in the air, mister!" and tugged at the front door.

"No! No lights, okay?" His urgent voice was barely a whisper. "Please, lady."

He was a tall and lanky silhouette against the faint light coming from the store a quarter-mile away. "If you'd just let me—"

"Officer . . " I had to fumble for his name. "Chapin, is it?"

It was the same game warden who'd been in court that afternoon. He peered at me closely.

"Oh *shit!*" he swore again. "Judge? Excuse me asking, ma'am, but what the hell are you doing *here?*"

"I live here," I answered. "At least, I'm staying here this week. More to the point, what the hell are *you* doing here?"

He stepped up onto the porch and pressed himself against the wall where the shadows were deepest. "Trying to save a few loons and swans. Mind pointing that thing somewhere else?"

"Oh. Sorry." I put the safety back on and laid the gun on the floor beside my chair.

"We got a tip that somebody down on this part of the island's been getting away with shooting loons for a few years now. Just stands on his porch and bangs away. If he bags one, it's just a few steps out and back in again before we can get a fix on where the gunshot came from. I decided that this year, by damn, I was gonna bag *him.*"

"You're talking about Mahlon Davis, aren't you?"

"Well, that's the way our suspicions have been running. Don't suppose you've seen him at it?"

"No-o, but—"

"But what, ma'am?"

"I was just remembering that both yesterday and today, I did hear gunshots when I first woke up. Didn't think anything about it, though."

"Not many people do, down here," he said bitterly. "It's the sound of springtime—spring peepers, migrating loons, shotgun blasts."

"Were you really going to spend the night under this porch?"

"I didn't know anybody was staying here, although I should have realized, the way your phone's been going crazy the last hour. I thought it belonged to somebody upstate that only comes down weekends. Stalking some of these boogers is like stalking wild turkeys. Except they're smarter and edgier than any turkey and they can spot a game warden a mile off. Only chance you have is to get in a place they can't see you and then grab 'em while the bird's still warm in their hands."

"Spoken like a man who enjoys his job," I laughed.

"We might not go in it for the sport," he said, "but most of us do like to hunt. And this surely is a hunt."

"Yeah, I used to hear tell of a revenuer like that. He'd lay out in the woods for a week at the time to catch somebody."

"It's not too bad. I've got a sleeping bag under there."

"Where's your car?"

"Parked up at the Shell Point ranger station. One of my buddies dropped me off up the road about forty minutes before you pulled in. Only thing I could think to do was dive under there before you saw me. I thought you'd go on to bed and I could just sneak out. How'd you spot me?"

"You were a little too liberal with your Off," I told him.

All this time, we'd been speaking in low tones. The wind was stiffening now and I was getting cold and suddenly quite tired.

I stood and pulled the windbreaker close around me. "Well, have fun. If I don't get to bed I won't be able to keep my eyes open in court tomorrow."

"Say, Judge?" Chapin's voice was diffident, but I knew that wheedling tone. God knows I'd heard it often enough from my brothers and nephews.

"No," I said.

"But we're both officers of the court, on the same side, aren't we?"

"Up to a point," I said. "If they were shooting loons for the hell of it, I'd say sure you could spend the night inside on the couch, but these people eat what they shoot and—"

"Most robbers spend what they steal," he said reasonably.

I sighed. "They're going to hate me."

"They won't even know it was you," he promised. "I'll slip out the back door. They won't know where I came from."

"You better not snore and I get first dibs on the bathroom," I told him.

He pulled his sleeping bag out from under the porch, shook it good, and we went inside, still not turning on any lights.

CHAPTER 8

Our life is like a stormy sea
Swept by the gales of sin and grief,
While on the windward and the lee
Hang heavy clouds of unbelief;
But o'er the deep a call we hear,
Like harbor bell's inviting voice;
It tells the lost that hope is near,
And bids the trembling soul rejoice.
"This way, this way, O heart oppress'd,
So long by storm and tempest driv'n;
This way, this way, lo, here is rest,"
Rings out the Harbor Bell of heaven.

—John H. Yates

When I awoke the next morning, it wasn't the sound of shotguns blasting across the water that floated through my window, but those very loud bantam gamecocks that Mickey Mantle keeps caged among the bushes at the edge of Mahlon's lot.

I'm sure he fights them somewhere on the island, but it was no concern of my mine. The clock said it was only six-ten, so I pulled the quilt over my head and tried to ignore their strident crows.

Less easy to ignore an hour later was the aroma of fresh-brewed coffee that worked its way under my closed door and down under the quilt till I was roused to pull a sweatshirt over my gown and go follow it out to the kitchen. Unfortunately, it turned out to be a phantom aroma for by the time I got there, the pot was empty, a cup was draining in the dish rack on the sink, and there was a note on the table:

6:45

Thanks for the loan of your couch. All quiet this a.m., so I'll try to sneak out without ruining your reputation.

Kidd Chapin

There were enough trees and bushes between the back door and the mobile home fifty feet away. With Clarence and his son away all week,

Chapin had a pretty good chance of succeeding unless someone happened to be looking right at the door the minute he opened it. Once outside and through the bushes, there was enough foot traffic back and forth between the road and the water, that no one would know if he were coming or going.

Reputation intact for one day more. My brothers would be pleased.

I showered while a fresh pot of coffee brewed, then slipped on jeans and sneakers and walked down to the water with that first hot cup cradled in my hands. The air was chilly and the wind was still off the water and stronger than last night, but the sun was burning off a light haze and it was going to be a beautiful day.

A door banged and I looked back to see young Guthrie standing there with books under his arm, his blond thatch brushed, dressed for school. He hesitated a moment, as if uncertain whether or not to acknowledge my presence. It was the first time I'd seen him since Sunday, but I greeted him casually and he joined me at the water's edge with some of his usual self-assurance.

"You laying out today?" he asked.

I smiled. "Wish I could."

"Me, too. I hate school."

"Yeah, I did, too."

He glanced over at me quickly before his eyes darted away again. "How'd you get to be a judge then?"

"I didn't say I hated learning. I said I hated school. Especially days like this. They made me want to be outdoors, not shut up inside."

"Yeah," he said, gazing wistfully out at the banks.

I found myself covertly examining his face and as much of his neck as was visible beneath the long-sleeved shirt, but I saw no fresh bruises. Just because Mahlon might use corporal punishment didn't make him a child abuser. My own daddy'd switched every one of us at one time or another for doing things not much worse than taking a boat without permission; but we never questioned his love for us. Unfortunately, there was no way to ask Guthrie if he felt loved and secure.

"Sometimes I have to say a courtroom feels like being back in school," I told him.

As if my words had given him the opening he'd needed, he said, "Want to thank you."

"For what?"

"My daddy told me he saw you yesterday and you let him off."

"I didn't let him off, son. The prosecution didn't prove its case."

He looked dubious but didn't comment.

More doors banged further up the path, near the road. Mark Lewis waved, then hopped in the car where his mother was waiting to drive him to school off-island. Another house over, Makely's mother, too, was already backing the car out of their garage. I've sat in too many juvenile courts to think that every woman who bears a child is *ipso facto* a loving mother out of a Hallmark commercial; nevertheless, seeing those two boys with their mothers made my heart ache for Guthrie, raised by a reclusive grandmother and a short-tempered grandfather.

If it bothered Guthrie, he didn't show it. Somewhere, not too far away, we heard a school bus horn.

"Reckon I better go." As he started up the path toward the road, he paused and said, "You ever get any clams? I told Mark and Makely to get you some."

(*"Another lie,"* sighed the preacher disapprovingly.)

(*"But think why,"* urged the pragmatist.)

"That was real thoughtful of you," I told Guthrie. "Thank you."

He nodded and hurried on. A moment later the big orange school bus gathered him up and rumbled on down the road.

As I lingered, Mahlon came out, cast a weather eye toward sky and water, then walked on down to where I stood.

"Getting ready to turn," he said. "Be raining by nightfall."

"With the sun this bright?"

"She can change quicker'n a woman's mind." He gave a sly, gap-toothed grin, but it was too early in the morning to annoy me.

"Well, looky yonder!" he said abruptly, pointing to a pair of water-fowl heading up the shoreline. "Loons!"

They passed us almost at eye level and less than fifty feet out. I'd never seen any up close and I was delighted by their beauty: soot-black heads, crisp black-and-white checkered backs. But there was something about their awkward silhouette—head lower than the humpbacked body, legs trailing along behind—that reminded me of a mourning dove's not-quite-got-it-together flight. They didn't seem to fly much faster than a dove either.

"Wisht I had my gun," said Mahlon.

"You'd shoot a loon in front of a judge?" I asked.

Again that sideways grin. "Ain't against the law to shoot at 'em. Only if you hit."

As the two loons disappeared into the distance, Mahlon followed their flight with a wistful yearning. "Lord, but they're a pretty sight."

"Then how come you shoot them?"

"Been doing it all my life," he said. "Mostly they come along the shoreline like them two, only a little farther out, right at the edge of your gun range, just teasing you. And it's sorta like they harden their feathers or something so the bird shot just slides off. I tell you, first time a youngun brings one home, he thinks he's a man sure enough."

Rites of passage may be important, "But they're an endangered species," I argued.

He gave an exasperated snort. "They ain't no more endangered than turtles and I wish to hell turtles ate people, then maybe some folks'd get some sense about it. Turtles and loons ain't endangered—*we're* the ones in danger."

With that, he stomped off toward the boat shed and a moment later I heard the steady pounding of his hammer.

⌘

The shoreline in front of the cottage is too narrow and too cluttered with rocks or piers to make walking any distance very pleasant, so I walked back up the path, left my cup on the porch, then cut through the Willis's side yard and hiked on up to Cab's, my favorite store on the island. In addition to Seven-Eleven type groceries and housewares, one side room of the store is devoted to heavy-duty fishing gear: rubber boots and waders, ropes and nets of all gauges, floats and sinkers of every size, clam rakes and flounder gigs; the other side room holds every kind of rod, reel, and lure known to man or fish, as well as electronic fish finders and other boat-related gadgets.

It's an education just to walk up and down the aisles and look at the six or eight different kinds of cotton, leather, nylon or rubber gloves—some thick for handling oysters, others heavy and rough-textured for dealing with slippery fish and eels.

It's also a place where an upstater can hear Down East locals gossiping with each other, once your ear ratchets up a notch to translate the rapid flow of that wonderful accent.

I bought an eastern edition of the *News and Observer* and was over by the T-shirts *("I'm Mommicked!"* said one), half eavesdropping and half reading the headlines, when someone said, "Morning, Judge."

It was Jay Hadley with a jug of milk in her hands.

"How's it going?" I said.

She hefted the jug. "Fine, if you don't count kids waiting for milk for their cereal."

I stepped back to let her pass, but she hesitated. "Look, I don't have time to talk right now, but you going to be at Andy's funeral this evening?"

"Remind me again when it is," I hedged.

She named a church on the west end of the island. "At four o'clock."

I told her I certainly hoped to be there if I could adjourn early.

"Good." She gave a brusque nod and hurried on up to the cash register.

As I drove out of the yard forty minutes later, Mahlon was still hard at work on the trawler. At Andy's house diagonally across the road, I noticed a patrol car and a pickup that belonged to one of the Bynum boys. Good thing Jay Hadley had reminded me about the funeral. My cousin Sue would appreciate it if I went.

"Sunshine along the Crystal Coast this morning," said the announcer on my radio, "with clouds moving in this afternoon. Fifty percent chance of rain, increasing to eighty percent by midnight."

Score another for Mahlon.

At the courthouse, when I popped my head into Chet's chambers, he said he planned to adjourn early, too. "Barbara Jean wants to go to the funeral."

"How is she this morning?" I asked.

His face was a bit drawn and his smile didn't quite reach all the way to his eyes when he said, "I hope you didn't take her seriously last night. She always lets Linville upset her for some reason."

"Well, I know how crazy she is about y'all's daughter," I said diplomatically.

"I've tried to stay out of it," he said with sudden determination, "but if Linville's going to keep bugging Barbara Jean . . . I swear to God I really wish Midge Pope'd gone on and lost that motel of his before he ever met Linville. Or if I'd blocked the sale of the Ritchie House, hell, she'd be waitressing out at the Sanitary right this minute."

"You really think so?"

"Naw, probably not. But that was the push she needed and without it, I honestly don't think she'd be where she is today, messing with Barbara Jean's head and getting her all wound up." He sighed. "The thing is, far as I'm concerned, it wouldn't be the end of the world if Barbara Jean *did* sell Neville Fishery. Jill doesn't want to run it. Her husband's a biologist with Duke's marine lab here. *He* doesn't want it."

"Your grandson?"

"He's one year old, for Christ's sake! Who knows what he'll be doing twenty years from now? I seriously doubt if it's messing with menhaden."

I thought how I'd feel if I had to sell Knott land. "But won't it kill Barbara Jean to give up her father's factory?"

"Only if it's to Linville Pope," he said grimly.

⌘

The morning session was mostly domestic. A young woman came forward and petitioned the court for an uncontested divorce. She was twenty-two, they had been married fourteen months according to the papers, and everything seemed in order.

"No children?" I asked, verifying the documents.

"No, ma'am," she answered softly.

"And no property?"

"No, ma'am." Her thin fingers pleated the soft floral pattern of her skirt.

I signed the papers. "Divorce granted."

She continued to stand there and gazed at me uncertainly. "Is that all there is?"

I know how she felt. Even if you run away with a man you've known less than seventy-two hours and get married on a whim by a magistrate you've never seen before, there are still vows to repeat, rings to exchange, a ritual. This child probably had the white veil and satin gown and six bridesmaids in pink tulle, with her mother and his lighting the candles from which they took flames and merged into one flame forever; and now, less than two years later, it came down to some legal papers filed and signed and a judge saying "Divorce granted."

"That's it?" she repeated.

"That's all," I said gently. "You're now legally divorced."

She walked out of the courtroom, still dazed.

⌘

At the lunch break, I didn't want to run into Lev at one of the waterfront restaurants and I was getting a little tired of fish twice a day anyhow, so I sneaked out to a salad bar at one of the fast-food places. To my surprise, Linville Pope was tucked into a corner booth alone.

She looked up with a pleased smile, moved aside some of the papers scattered across the table and invited me to join her.

When I observed that one wouldn't expect to find her at a Shoney's, she grimaced and said, "I hope you are right. Some nut has found my usual lunch spot and keeps making scenes. It seems easier to eat here till he gets over it."

"Zeke Myers?" I asked, spreading alfalfa sprouts across the top of my salad.

Her eyebrows lifted. "Do you know him?"

"No, but I was in the Ritchie House Monday and heard him shouting. Something about a boat?"

"Oh yes. It was indeed about a boat." Her small fingers tore a hot roll into neat pieces and she buttered one very precisely. "But I do not want to bore you."

When I assured her she wouldn't, she told me about the large cabin cruiser she and her husband had bought down in Florida.

"Midge wanted to run day trips out to the Cape or take small private parties out to the Gulf Stream for a day of fishing, but it did not work out—my husband was never well enough to outfit it—and the boat is much too big for me to run alone, so I sold it to Zeke Myers, who thought he could make a go of it. He bought it as is and he got a very fine bargain, whatever he may think at the moment."

She swallowed the morsel of roll and began to butter another, as I lifted a lettuce leaf in search of a third black olive.

"So why's he so mad?"

"Because when he went to get a commercial license for the boat, he discovered that it had been built in Taiwan."

I still didn't see the problem.

"It seems there are federal cabotage laws in this country which prevent a foreign-built boat from being used for commercial purposes in domestic waters. Something to do with protection of jobs in our own boatyards perhaps?"

She said it without much interest. I thought of how much money Zeke Myers must have paid even for a "very fine bargain."

Setting down my glass of iced tea, I said, "No wonder he's angry."

She shrugged. "There are solutions if he would explore the possibilities, but he is having too much fun feeling that I screwed him over."

"Didn't you?"

Her lips curved in a cat-in-the-cream-pitcher smile. "Maybe I did," she said candidly. "But not fatally. Instead of following me around town and harassing me, if he would spend half that energy on the phone to his congressman, he could ask him to originate a private bill in the House and get an exception from the cabotage restrictions. They do it all the time, I am told. It may take him a little time and aggravation, but in the end, he could have the license he needs. That is what my husband would have done once we found out about the law."

"Do you by any chance play chess?" I asked.

"No, I never had time for board games," she said. "I would rather play for real."

"You mean for money."

"Why not? Having money is another way to keep score and a lot more fun than not having it. Power is even better, of course." A shadow crossed her placid face as she pushed her plate aside and centered her tea on the table before her. A memory from earlier years of subordination?

"Be honest," she said. "Why else did you become a judge?"

"I thought I could make a difference," I answered primly. "For the greater good."

"So do we all, Deborah. So do we all." She leaned her head back against the booth and her fine ash-blonde hair fell away from her face to accentuate the delicate skull just beneath her fair skin. "That is ninety-nine percent of the problem down here: everybody thinks they know what is best for everyone else. It would be amusing if it were not so sad."

"And if it weren't messing with people's livelihoods," I added tartly.

"It is not messing with livelihoods," she corrected me gently. "No, no. It is messing with power. Every one of those people who are so vocal could find other ways to earn a living. They just do not want to. They are like the spotted owl loggers. They want to go on doing what they are used to doing. What their fathers were used to doing. Without one single change, even though the changes I am working toward will profit everyone in the long run and maybe even raise their quality of life. Look at your friend Barbara Jean. If she would sell to me tomorrow, I would give her half again what Neville Fishery is actually worth and she could walk away from all this controversy a very well-to-do lady. But she will not. And why?"

"Power?" I asked, playing the part she'd cast me in.

Linville leaned forward, her fingers laced around her tea.

"Well, what would she be if she did not have the fishery? What would she be in charge of? Money cannot *begin* to replace the psychic satisfaction she must get out of signing paychecks for twenty-three black men and a half-dozen whites. They give her respect. Their families give her respect. People pay attention when she speaks out at a hearing. She will never give that up of her own free will. Not for mere money."

I sat back from my plate. "So you'll coerce her? She told me you've threatened to build a boat storage facility on Harkers Island, right next door to her daughter."

"I do not threaten, Deborah. I merely state. Besides, it will be a very nice facility. Landscaped. Screened with flowering bushes. It will not be an eyesore. Honest." Again that quiet complacent smile. "Assuming, that is, that she chooses to let me go ahead with it. If her husband cannot talk her out of it."

"What about Andy Bynum?" I asked suddenly.

She made a dismissive motion with her slender hands. "Another who enjoyed power. He could stand in the door of his fish house and take or reject whatever a waterman offered him. He liked running that Independent Fishers Alliance because it gave him a forum to impose his will on the rest of us. Or to try."

Her pager went off. She frowned at the number displayed, glanced at her delicate gold watch, and said, "Too bad. I wanted to hear about you and Levi Schuster, but it seems I have to go now."

"Nothing to hear." I gave a dismissive motion of my own. "We used to be together a zillion years ago."

"Last night meant nothing?"

"We might've stirred some old ashes," I admitted.

"And found a few hot coals?"

I shook my head.

("Liar!" whispered the preacher.)

"Then you will not mind if I—?"

"Would it matter?"

She laughed. "Probably not. Still . . ."

"Be my guest."

("You're gonna be sorry you said that," warned the pragmatist.)

⌘

As it turned out, there were so many requests for continuances in the afternoon session that we were finished for the day a few minutes before three. I quickly adjourned and headed back for Harkers Island. Dark clouds were rolling in from the west and rain that had been predicted didn't seem far away.

By the time I got to the church where Andy's funeral was to be preached, it was nearly packed to the brim. There were Sunday school classrooms on either side of the main sanctuary, though, and folding panels slid back so that another fifty people could be shoehorned in. I was among them. People who came even later had to stand along the back walls.

The casket was closed before the family entered—Andy's two sons, their wives, five grandchildren, and a handful of people who could have been brothers and sisters or cousins. Seated on the side as I was, I had a good view. The daughters-in-law had red-rimmed eyes and the boys looked as if they'd done their share of mourning, too. An older woman cried silently through the whole service.

Chet and Barbara Jean sat amid a group of members of the Alliance. Or so I assumed, since at least half of them, including Barbara Jean and Jay Hadley, wore white carnations in their lapels. Two teenagers sat beside Jay. The girl looked to be seventeen or eighteen and was a younger, prettier version of her blonde mother. I'd heard the boy was only sixteen, but he had a man's growth and was darker of hair and eyes.

The choir sang "Rock of Ages" and "Safe in the Arms of Jesus," then the preacher called for prayer. He was on the charismatic side and got so carried away with such a huge audience that, at one point, he seemed to think he was conducting a revival instead of a funeral. As he spoke of repentance and salvation and exhorted us to save our souls ("For ye knoweth not the hour when the Lord shall call ye home"), I almost expected him to issue an invitation and for the pianist to break into "Almost Persuaded."

At the last minute, however, he restrained himself and settled into an earnest detailing of Andy Bynum's goodness and virtues and the legacy of love and respect he was leaving behind, "a monument not carved in stone, my friends, nor writ in water, but indelibly etched on the hearts and lives of people he touched."

Near the end, he alluded to the manner in which death had come and said, "Andy's boys, Drew and Maxton, asks y'all to search your memories of last Sunday. If anybody passed Andy out there near the banks, if anybody saw someone else out there—if you don't want to tell the sheriff, at least find it in your heart to tell one of them."

A final hymn, a prayer, then we rose and followed the casket out to the churchyard where a blue tent protected three rows of folding chairs and the open grave. The casket was rolled into place and the family was seated while the rest of us stood quietly and hoped the rain would hold off a half hour longer.

After another homily and another prayer, the preacher shook the hand of each family member and they went back inside the church to wait until the casket had been lowered, the dirt shoveled back in, and the wreaths arranged to cover the raw earth.

The congregation sort of shifted away from the graveside, too, as if it weren't quite good manners to stand and stare while this was going on. Car doors slammed as some people left immediately. Most, though, lingered in small groups to shake their heads over Andy's murder and to wonder aloud what would happen to the Alliance now. I saw Telford Hudpeth talking to Barbara Jean and Jay Hadley. Chet was in deep conversation with someone I didn't recognize.

Detective Quig Smith was there with Deputy Marvin Willitt, who was in uniform.

"Gentlemen," I said.

"Ma'am," said Deputy Willitt and immediately cut out.

"Was it something I said?" I asked.

Smith grinned, "Nah, he's supposed to be directing traffic."

"Really?"

"Okay, and asking a few questions, too. Making himself available in case somebody takes to heart what the preacher was saying." He glanced over to where two laborers from the funeral home were shoveling dirt. "You ever been to New Orleans?"

"That's an odd question."

"I was just thinking about the difference in water tables. How they have to bury their dead above ground. Not like here." He shook his head. "Going to be hard keeping developers out of this place. Too much high ground over here."

It looked pretty flat to me, but I suppose these things are relative.

We were standing at the edge of the crowd, two virtual outsiders. As long as we were alone, I felt free to say, "From what the sons are asking, I gather that there's been no progress toward finding Andy's killer?"

"Wouldn't say that exactly. We've been up and down the island asking questions, especially houses on the sound side. People can be right vague about what they've seen."

"But somebody did see something?"

He rubbed his chin. "Now, Judge."

As we spoke, his denim-blue eyes roved the crowd and he nodded courteously whenever anyone made eye contact. "You're staying in that little yellow house behind Clarence Willis, right?"

"Yes. It belongs to my cousins."

"They ever have anything stolen?"

"Not that I—well, maybe a couple of spinner reels. A tape player, stuff like that."

"He file a report?"

"No. He figured he knew who took it and it was never all that much."

"Mickey Mantle Davis, hmm?"

"He did use to be right bad for taking stuff that wasn't nailed down," I admitted.

"Still is," said Smith with a slow smile that told me he'd heard about a hand puppet accusing Mickey Mantle of bicycle theft.

"But that's from off-islanders, and once my cousins got some decent window locks, it pretty much stopped. Mickey Mantle would never bust a window on them."

"How long you known the Winberrys?" he asked abruptly.

"You *do* jump around, don't you? Is this relevant to something?"

"Just wondering. Somebody said you went to a party with them the other night. I guess judges hang out a lot together though."

"No more than sheriff's deputies," I said.

As if to disprove my point, Chet picked that minute to walk over and ask if I'd like to ride in to Beaufort with them for dinner. "One of us could run you back across by boat later."

"Thanks, Chet, but it looks like rain and I think I'll make it an early night tonight," I told him.

As he walked away to collect Barbara Jean, who seemed to be having a strategy meeting with several of her colleagues, I saw that Quig Smith was smiling again.

"What?" I asked.

"Just thinking about late nights and such. How well you know Kidd Chapin?"

I grinned. "More to the point, Detective Smith, how well do *you* know him?"

"He's a catbird, ol' Kidd. But I'll say this for him: he's a fine lawman. Real big on conservation, too." He gave me a considering look. "I bet you're not married either."

"That's it," I laughed and turned toward my car, but Smith fell in step beside me.

"The first road through the island was paved with seashells," he confided. "You wouldn't believe the pile of shells used to be off Shell Point."

"Where Indians used to come to the island every spring and pig out on oysters and clams," I said. "I know. I've heard the stories."

"They say there were so many shells it was like they were trying to build a causeway out to the cape." He kicked at the pavement consideringly. "Been better off to've kept this road in shells. Runoff from asphalt's something awful. We ought to pass a law that for every twenty-five parking spaces, parking lots've got to have at least one deciduous tree. Because even if it's clean rainwater—which it never is—too much fresh water can be just as bad for estuarine life as polluted water."

"Well," I said heartily when we reached my car, "it's certainly been nice talking to you and—"

He leaned closer. "Kidd said if I saw you to ask if you like black olives or green peppers on your pizza."

"I beg your pardon?"

"Kidd said—"

"No," I interrupted. "I heard that part. You tell Officer Chapin that I said No way, José."

Smith rubbed his chin dubiously. "Well, I'll tell him, but you know what's going to happen, don't you?"

"What?"

"You're probably going to get olives *and* peppers."

"You tell Kidd Chapin that if he shows up at my place, I'm going to turn on every light and blow a horn so that everybody in the neighborhood knows he's there."

"Generally they ring a church bell," Smith chuckled. "You hear a church bell ringing on a weekday in the spring, you can bet there's a game warden on the island."

⌘

Back at the cottage, I waved to Mahlon and Guthrie, who were still out working on the boat. Considering that Mahlon hoped to hold the Bynum boys to Andy's promise of that truck engine, I was surprised he'd skipped the funeral. I slipped off my dress and got into jeans and a slouchy sweatshirt, thinking I'd go over and watch, but a car pulled up outside and I heard the door slam.

It was Jay Hadley, still dressed for the funeral in a soft navy suit and red-and-white spectator pumps with a red purse. A far cry from the shirt and shorts she'd worn on Sunday. She carried a bulging manila folder.

When I went to the door, she said, "Sorry to bother you, Judge, but I need a little advice, if you don't mind."

I invited her in and offered her something to drink, but all she would take was a glass of ice water.

"You see, Judge—"

"Please. Call me Deborah."

Until then, she'd been business-like. Now she looked downright shy. "And I'm Jay."

That out of the way, I asked how I could help and she laid the manila folder on the couch between us.

"These are some of Andy's papers. See, the Alliance wants me to act as interim president and I said I would. Andy's boy, Maxton, brought me over a big stack of stuff last night and when I was going through it—" She hesitated. "I don't know if Barbara Jean Winberry's told you how much Andy hated Linville Pope?"

"I gather they didn't get along very well, but I don't know any details."

"Andy's had it in for her ever since she wrecked his honey pot over on North River about a year ago."

I couldn't help smiling as I remembered Andy talking about his honey pot.

She gave a sad smile back and pushed away a lock of sun-bleached hair that had fallen into her eyes. "When there were no other oysters around, when nobody could find a half-box of crabs, Andy'd go progging around a place on North River and always bring home a nice mess for supper. Linville Pope helped develop a stretch right slam on his honey pot and that was the end of that. He was iller than a channel crab over it, and after that, seems like he was always out to get back at her."

I could understand. From what I've heard most watermen are secretive and protective of their special good luck places.

"Anyhow, 'bout a week ago, or maybe two weeks, Andy said he'd finally got the goods on her. 'She's built her house on sand,' he said, and he was going to blow it down."

"He was vindictive?"

"Andy Bynum was one of the decentest men on the island and he did everything by the rules, but if you ever got on his bad side, he'd use the rules to get you back."

"He didn't tell you what the goods were?"

"No, but I know he spent a lot of time at the courthouse, messing in the public records. That's what this is," she said, patting the file folder. "His notes, the copies he made of her permits, newspaper stories and a bunch of other stuff. The thing is, I've been through it and if there's something there, I can't see it. You're a lawyer. Maybe you could spot it."

"For what purpose?" I asked.

"Linville Pope's getting to be very strong in the area," Jay said frankly. "She doesn't mind cutting corners to get what she wants. And what she wants is all commercial fishing out of the sound. I think it'd be good if we could clip her wings just enough to even things out."

Much as I was starting to come down on the side of the watermen, I wasn't easy about blackmail and coercion. On the other hand, if Linville really had done something illegal, why should she profit by it at their expense?

"Okay," I said, taking the folder. "We'll see if she broke any of the rules."

"Thanks," she said. "Deborah."

"You're welcome, Jay."

⌘

The rain finally set in for real around dark and it rained so hard for a couple of hours that I had to go around closing windows.

I only meant to just leaf through the folder and then go find something to eat, once the rain slacked. But I got absorbed in all the land deals Pope Properties had been involved in, and the next time I looked up, it was nearly ten p.m.

Every eating place on the island would be closed by now.

I'd left a side window cracked for ventilation and realized that somewhere, someone was cooking something that smelled luscious. Something with olive oil and garlic and—

A low voice outside the window said, "Your pizza's here."

CHAPTER 9

Ever present, truest Friend,
Ever near Thine aid to lend,
Leave us not to doubt and fear,
Groping on in darkness drear,
When the storms are raging sore,
Hearts grow faint, and hopes give o'er,
Whisper softly, "Wanderer, come!
Follow Me, I'll guide thee home."

—Marcus M. Wells

"This is absolutely, positively the last time," I told Kidd Chapin as I reached for a second slice of the best pizza I'd eaten in six months. Not only did it have olives and peppers and sausage, two slices even had anchovies, an irresistible combination. "If you don't catch somebody shooting loons tomorrow morning, you'll have to go back under the porch or lie out in the bushes.

"And get my tailfeathers shot off?" he grinned. "Not!"

"Well, it won't be here," I warned, "because I'll finish up tomorrow evening and drive on back to Dobbs."

We were seated at the Formica kitchen table, shades drawn, splitting the last three beers in the refrigerator, and telling war stories.

At least Kidd Chapin was. He reminded me of Terry Wilson, my SBI buddy. I'd already heard his oystering story about the poachers he'd caught only that day—two old-timers who swore on their mothers' graves that they'd harvested that bushel of succulent bivalves before the thirty-first of March, the day oyster season officially closed. "They said they were just bringing those two-week-old sackfuls out in their boat to wet 'em down again."

Next had come his bear story, two loon stories, and now we were onto spot-lighting deer.

"—so we're trying to sneak up on this abandoned house out at the edge of a soybean field where we've heard there's been lights flashing around at night and the sound of gunshots. Well, just about the time we get in range, the door flings open and this powerful flashlight beam sweeps across the field and then pow-pow-pow! We dive for cover and land in a briar-covered ditch with about six inches of water. A minute later, we hear the little skinny one yell, 'I b'lieve I got him, Cletus!'

"Ray and me, we raise up real easy like and see this man mountain come to the door—bushy red beard, carrying this humongous bowie knife and wearing a tee shirt that says 'Kill 'Em All And Let God Sort It Out.' He's one mean-looking mother. 'Where?' he says.

"'Over yonder,' says the skinny one, and he's laughing and whooping like he's killed a bear, and here come that flashlight beam again.

He savored an olive and took a deep swallow of beer.

"Now Ray and me, we've got these riot shotguns, so I shout, 'State Wildlife Officer! Throw down your gun!' The big guy runs back inside, but the little guy's not quite sure what to do. 'Bout that time, Ray pumps a shell into the chamber and soon as he hears that, the little guy throws down his gun and hits the dirt, yelling, 'I ain't done nothing.'

"I run around to the back of the house about the time the door opens and I think for sure I'm gonna see the snout of an M-16 or something. Instead, here comes Man Mountain's nose, real cautious-like, and this little teeny voice says, 'Who's there?' like he's expecting the Avon lady.

"I tell him to come on out with his hands up and it's 'Yessir! Yessir! Don't shoot.'

"So we get 'em handcuffed, under arrest, down on their knees and all the time they're swearing they ain't done a thing. 'Course Ray and me, we know they have, so we start gathering up the evidence and the first thing we find is this shotgun shell. Only it's birdshot, nothing that'd bring down a deer. About twenty yards out, we finally find what the little guy was shooting at. Not a deer. A goddamned house cat!

"I mean, here we are: two officers with riot guns, two guys hand-cuffed and under arrest, and one mangy dead *Felis domesticus,* which, you being a judge, you know is not against the law to shoot."

"So what'd you do?" I asked, licking tomato sauce from my fingers.

"Only thing I can do." He grinned and reached for the last piece of pizza. "I pick up that dead cat and I shake it in their faces and yell, 'You sorry piece of garbage, you see this?'

"And the little one starts whining, 'Yessir, please sir, I didn't mean to do it.'

"'You know this is against the law, don't you?'

"And the big one's moaning, 'Yessir. We're sorry. We won't never do it again. I promise you, sir!'

"'Okay,' I say, 'We'll let you off this time, but we catch you shooting cats again, you're gonna be in a heap of trouble.'"

Laughing, I topped his glass from the last bottle of beer and poured the rest into my own. "And cat lovers everywhere salute you, sir!"

"'Course, we actually did see some guys spot-lighting deer a couple of nights later. We eased my state-issue Bronco down into this driveway on a country road and parked facing out. No lights on in the house, people had gone to bed. And we sit there about an hour till sure 'nuff, here comes a pickup with two jokers sitting out there on the front fenders. One's working the spotlight and the other has the gun. Well, we scrunch way down in the seat till after they pass, then I switch on the ignition and try to follow them and all of a sudden the whole right side of my Bronco sags down. We got out and find two of our tires melted slam down on the rims. Seems that old farmer was in the habit of dumping his hot coals and ashes in the driveway before he made up the fire and went to bed at night."

"Bet you had fun explaining that to your boss," I said as he cleared away the box and paper plates and put the beer bottles in a recycling bag.

"Well, tell you the truth, I could never exactly find the right time to break it to him so I just stole the spares off'n a couple of other officers' Broncos."

While I washed our glasses and wiped down the surfaces, he swept the floor.

"You're right handy around the house," I commented, spreading the dish towel to dry over the drainer.

"Never been too hung up about the difference between women's work and men's," he said with an easy smile. "Not since I learned about oysters."

"What about oysters?" I asked suspiciously.

"They flip-flop back and forth on their gender, depending on who's on top. Grow the lady on top of the gentleman, and a few months later, he'll be female, she'll be male and they'll still get baby oysters."

"You're making that up," I told him.

"There's a field guide to seashells in the living room," he said. "If you don't believe me, go check it out."

I went and found the book and looked up oysters. After a paragraph or two detailing how oysters grow in the marshes and mud flats of intertidal zones where water movement is gentle, the entry finally got down to their sex life. Guess what?

"You sure you don't want to stay on down over the weekend?" he asked.

"Positive. Not that it hasn't been fun."

He gave me a considering look.

"Forget it," I told him. "We're not oysters."

I went to bed.

Alone.

⌘

Along about two a.m., I woke up thirsty from the anchovies and tiptoed out to the kitchen for a drink of water.

And realized that thirst wasn't what had waked me.

Kidd Chapin was a dark shape at the back window and I saw him motion for silence through the faint reflected light from up at the store. Outside, a light rain was still falling. The wet live oaks swayed in a strong southwest wind and made moving shadows everywhere. I could hear low waves breaking upon the sand; and every fifteen seconds, a faint gleam from the lighthouse swept through the window over on the east side.

I stood on tiptoe to peer over Kidd's shoulder, past the bushes, to the road, and whispered in his ear, "What are we looking at?"

"I'm not sure. I went to the bathroom about ten minutes ago and happened to look out and see somebody coming up from the water."

"Fishermen use the path all times of the night and day," I told him, "depending on what's running and how the wind's blowing or—"

"I know about the wind and spring tides, Ms. Judge," he reminded me.

"Sorry."

"Besides, he didn't walk straight on up the path and down the road like a waterman. He kept so far in the shadows I never did get a clear look. In fact if it weren't that you never see any blacks on the island, I couldn't know if he was black or white. He slipped through those bushes and on across the road and now I don't see him anymore."

"What'd he have on?"

"I don't know. It was all dark. Probably a jacket with a hood on it."

"Maybe you ought to call Marvin Willitt," I said.

"What for?"

"You just said—"

"Yeah, and I tell Marvin Willitt where I am and half of Harkers Island'll know it by daybreak. And what if it's somebody only just out cheating on his wife, trying not to be seen by *her* husband?"

"'Only just out cheating on his wife?'" I couldn't help the snide acid.

"Hey, I'm not condoning it, just recognizing the facts, ma'am."

He stepped back from the window as I opened the refrigerator and squinted against the sudden bright light. "You want a glass of tomato juice?"

"Okay."

We took our glasses back toward the unlit living room. A stiff April wind was pouring through the south windows straight off the water, thick with rain and salt and funky seaside odors. I shivered in my thin gown.

"Aw, don't go back to bed yet," said Kidd. "Is it too cold for you? I'll put the windows down."

"No, I like it, but I have to put on something warmer."

"My sleeping bag zips open to a double comforter," he offered and I saw white teeth flash in the near darkness.

"I'd hate for you to disfurnish yourself," I said dryly and went into my room to slip on a fleecy sweatshirt and slippers and to lay hands on a comforter of my own.

As I pulled the shirt over my head, I noticed through the window a flicker of light over at Andy's house. I quickly stuffed my gown inside a pair of warm-up pants, kicked off the slippers and pulled on sneakers, then hurried out to Kidd.

"It's Andy Bynum's house," I said. "The man that was killed Sunday? Somebody's sneaking around his house."

"Hey, wait a minute!" he rasped as I slid open the door. "Where do you think you're—"

"It's okay," I assure him, jingling my car keys. "I've got a gun in my trunk, remember?"

He grabbed my arm before I stepped off the porch into the rain and held me while he crammed his feet in his own shoes. "Now listen up, Ms. Judge—no guns. You stay here and I'll go—"

I yanked my arm free with a low snarl. "I've got a better idea, Officer Chapin. *You* stay here and call Marvin Willitt and I'll go."

"Or," he amended, "we can go together, only no gun, okay?"

I nodded and we set off through the bushes. Between the security light near Mark's house and the lights up at the store, we didn't need a flashlight to see where we were going, but we were keeping to the shadows as much as possible ourselves and there was a certain amount of stumbling so that we wound up running across the rain-slick road hand in hand, then melted into the bushes beneath the front windows of Andy Bynum's house.

Unlike Sue and Carl's little yellow clapboard vacation cottage, this was a year-round brick home, solid and comfortable, with blinds and drapes at all the windows. Yet the window of the front door was uncurtained and we could see the glow of a moving flashlight inside.

"Stay here," said Kidd as he moved onto the porch. "Please?"

As I may have said before, I don't mind letting men do my dirty work if it makes them feel good, but that doesn't include using one as a body shield. On the other hand, this one seemed to have picked up a short piece of pipe on our way over and I certainly didn't need to be in the middle if he started swinging it.

The front door was unlatched, but when Kidd pushed, it swung inward with a horrendous squeak and the light immediately vanished. As he stepped inside, I remembered that there was a side door I could be usefully watching, but for the moment, I blanked on which side. By the time I'd circled all the way around the house, the door was standing wide open and I saw a dark shape fleeing for the water. From the angle he was taking, I had a feeling he'd tied up at Mahlon's landing, so I cut through the Lewis's yard, trying not to skid on the wet grass, and sprinted down the narrow footpath the boys had worn through that overgrown vacant field, down to the shoreline. I bet I'd have made it in time to get a good look at the intruder, too, only just before I was to break through the bank, the toe of my sneaker caught in one of Mahlon's discarded stop nets and I went sprawling into a yucca plant.

A stiff needled blade jabbed my cheek, another raked my forehead, and more impaled themselves in my head and hands. I disentangled myself as quickly as I could, but already I could hear the boat motor; and when I finally made it to the shore, all I saw were the running lights as it headed out to the channel and back toward Beaufort. Without moon or stars, I couldn't even say if it had a cabin or an open cockpit, for it was just a gray blur against the dark water.

Discouraged, thoroughly wet and hurting like hell, I started to cross Mahlon's rickety dock and stumbled against a bucket. It went banging against the piling and, as I set it upright, a light snapped on. Mahlon's grizzled head appeared at the open window and he squinted out to see into the darkness.

"Who's that out there?"

"It's just me, Mahlon," I called, edging away from the light. "I couldn't sleep and was taking a walk and I kicked a bucket. Sorry. G'night."

He was still muttering about dingbatters without enough sense to come in out of the rain as I walked hastily back to the cottage.

Kidd Chapin was there before me and as soon as I stepped inside, he drew the shades and turned on the lights. His wet hair clung flat to his head, but mine was hanging in strings.

"Sweet Jesus in the morning! Look at you. What happened?"

I touched my damp face and my torn hands came away with more blood. "I fell into a damn yucca."

"Spanish bayonets," he said, calling its colloquial name.

"They weren't kidding. The way it hurts, I'm lucky I didn't get one in the eye. I don't suppose you got a look at him either?"

"No, by the time I got to the open side door, you were both gone and I didn't have a clue which way. I was on my way to the water when the light came on over there and I could see you by yourself, so I decided to sneak on back in here while you were creating a diversion. Come on, Ms. Judge, let's get you cleaned up."

I was drained into docility and obediently sat at the kitchen table while he washed the blood off my face and hands with a hot soapy washcloth, then dabbed at the cuts and punctures with peroxide.

"Hope you got a light calendar tomorrow," he said. "You're going to look like hell a couple of days, but I'd leave the Band-Aids off, let the air heal it."

"Take two aspirin and call you tomorrow?" I said groggily.

"Wouldn't hurt."

"Which?"

"Both."

I swallowed the aspirin he brought me, shucked off the wet sweatshirt and warm-up pants, and crawled into bed.

⌘

My head felt as if it'd barely touched the pillow when Kidd's hand touched my bare shoulder. At first I thought it was still that hazy cusp between night and sunrise, but according to the clock it was nearly seven-thirty and I realized that the gray light was due to the gray day. The rain had stopped, though clouds still lingered. If more clouds didn't blow in, it would probably be sunny by noon. I tried to sit up and every muscle in my body started screaming that this was really a bad idea and maybe we could all come back and try it again tomorrow.

"I didn't want to leave without saying goodbye," said Kidd.

"No loons?"

"No. Ol' Mahlon left at first light without a gun. Gone fishing, I'd guess."

A hot cup of coffee steamed on the stand beside the bed. I eased up against the pillows and took a grateful sip.

"How'd you know I like it black?"

"No sugar bowl on the counter, no milk in the fridge. Made it easy. How you feeling?"

"Stiff, sore. How do I look?"

"Beautiful," he said. "Except for the dueling scars. You're a gutsy lady. Want to come hunting poachers with me some night?"

"Any time you're in Dobbs," I smiled.

"Bet you just would, too. Listen, though. You were too beat to talk, but whoever that was last night, he must have gone straight to the desk in what looked like the den 'cause when I walked in, it was flat torn apart. Papers everywhere. I called Quig Smith and told him and he's coming out this morning to see if he can get any fingerprints off the doors and desk. I didn't touch anything inside and you never went in, so he's going to tell Bynum's family that he got an anonymous phone tip, okay?"

"Okay," I yawned.

Very gently, he leaned over and kissed my uninjured cheek. "See you around, Ms. Judge," and then he was gone.

⌘

A hot shower did wonders for my aching muscles, but it also brought out the bright red of my scratches. I hesitated between leaving them clean for quicker healing and covering them with makeup.

Vanity won, but I promised my face I'd take cream and face soap with me and wipe off all the makeup as soon as court was adjourned. That should be by noon or one o'clock and nothing was on the docket for next day.

And all the time I was dressing, Kidd's words rang in my head. What sort of burglar tore apart a desk and scattered papers rather than grabbing up the nearest pawnable items? And did he want papers relating to the Alliance or papers relating to Pope Properties?

Suddenly I was reevaluating the figure I'd chased last night. Could it have been a woman? More specifically, Linville Pope? Barbara Jean's accusations began to take on a tinge of reality.

Since it would be almost as quick to swing back past the island as to leave straight for Beaufort, I planned to wait till after court to pack and clean up. Unless Jay Hadley told (and why would she?), no one else knew I had half of Andy's papers; but I've always thought it better to set the glass back on a sturdy table than cry over spilt milk, even though the cottage offered few places to hide a bundle of files. I briefly considered and rejected the linen closet with its neat stacks of sheets and towels, the oven, or between the mattresses.

In the end, I went for Poe's solution. Neatly stacked for recycling beside the kitchen garbage basket were all the newspapers I'd read that week, both the *News and Observer* and the *Carteret County News-Times*. Quickly, I divided the files between several of the newspapers, replaced them in the stack, and convinced myself that no one would give the papers a second glance.

Outside, grinding gears announced the arrival of a large white truck in the field next to Mahlon's. The door panel read COASTAL WASTE MANAGEMENT CORP, MOREHEAD CITY. Two muscular men stepped out, surveyed the scope of the job, then began tossing junk into the back of the truck. I saw Mickey Mantle go over and speak to them, then a few minutes later, he was tugging at those gamecock pens and moving them one at a time back nearer the house.

Looked like Linville Pope was serious about cleaning up her property. What was it she'd said yesterday? "I do not threaten. I merely state."

No joke.

⌘

As I crossed the causeway to the mainland, I passed Quig Smith and he gave me a big wave.

At the courthouse, Chet did a double take when he saw my face. "My God, girl! You look like you ought to be standing in front of the bench instead of sitting on it."

"Oh come on, it doesn't look that bad, does it?" I examined my face again in the mirror. My hair half hid the scratch on my forehead and makeup almost covered the deeper one on my cheek.

He shook his head. "What happened?"

"I fell into a yucca plant."

"Ouch!" He flinched in sympathy. "Just jumped up and bit you, huh?"

"What I get for playing Nancy Drew," I said and told him about chasing the burglar who'd broken into Andy Bynum's house. With some editing, of course. I didn't need stories getting back to my family, and he didn't need to know about the papers or Kidd Chapin either, which meant I had to fudge about what Quig Smith knew.

"I hope you won't mention this to anybody. I didn't want to get hung up down here, maybe have to stay over an extra day to answer dumb questions, so I didn't give my name when I reported it," I lied.

"You're lucky they didn't take a shot at you. Would you know him if you saw him again?"

I shook my head. "I'm not even sure if it was a man or a woman."

"What about Mahlon Davis or Mickey Mantle?"

"You know them?"

"Everybody knows them. They've never showed up in my courtroom yet. Probably just a matter of time. Although, to give the devil his due, they're both brilliant woodworkers, even if they are morally retarded. Mickey Mantle did some cabinet work for us last fall. Long as we could keep him sober . . ."

"Yeah. It wasn't Mahlon, though, because he was home in bed. But that reminds me. Before I leave this time, I need to speak to somebody in Social Services about his grandson Guthrie. I want to know if Mahlon treats him too rough."

"That'd be Shelby Spivey. And she probably already has a file started on him if he lives with Mahlon."

131

I made a note of the name and number, as Chet glanced at his watch and stood to go to his courtroom.

"What happened to *you?*" I said, noticing how he favored his right leg.

"Pulled a muscle when I jogged up for my paper this morning." He grinned. "We're the walking wounded, aren't we, girl? I'll be finished by mid-morning, so in case I don't see you 'fore you leave—" He gave me a warm hug. "Drive careful and come back real soon, you hear?"

"Thanks, Chet. Say 'bye to Barbara Jean for me. I hope it all works out about the fishery."

⌘

Chet may have been finished by mid-morning, but I wasn't far behind. When the last judgment had been rendered and the last paper signed, I stopped by the Clerk of Court's office to thank her for her courtesies and to see if there were any last-minute details I'd missed before I left.

Darlene Leonard laughed as I entered. "Well, speak of the Devil and up she jumps!"

"Somebody been taking my name in vain?" I asked.

She said she'd just hung up from talking to the chief district court judge and he'd spoken to *my* chief, who said, and I quote: "We'll bring Harrison Hobart out of retirement to handle Judge Knott's schedule here next week, so, yes, you can keep her an extra week."

Just like that. Not "Do you want to?" Not "Would you mind?"

(*"What'd you do to tick off F. Roger Longmire?"* asked the pragmatist, who usually kept track of where I stood with my district's chief judge.)

(*"It must have been that smartass remark you made about his brown shoes last week,"* said the preacher. *"One of these days you're gonna learn—"*)

Before I could work up a good head of steam, Darlene Leonard said, "Judge Longmire sent word for you to get a good rest and enjoy the beach next week. He said you've earned it."

So much for pragmatism and preaching.

With the folders Jay Hadley had given me still uppermost in my mind, I asked, "You knew Andy Bynum, didn't you?"

"I knew who he was," she answered, "but I can't say I really knew him."

"Someone said he'd been digging through some old deeds and such. Would you have helped him?"

"No, that would have been over at the Register of Deeds," she said and gave me directions to the office.

There, a helpful young clerk remembered Andy clearly. "Sure, Mr. Bynum was in and out almost every day right up till about a week before he was killed. Wasn't it just awful? He was such a nice man."

She had no idea what he was after specifically, "But he started with a piece of property Mrs. Pope had acquired over on Harkers Island last month and pulled most everything he could find on Pope Properties, right back to when she handled the sale of the Ritchie House."

"Which piece of Harkers Island property?" I asked.

She very nicely pulled out the right deed book on her first try. As I'd suspected, it was the land adjacent to Chet and Barbara Jean's daughter, formerly owned by one Gilbert Epson. So Andy had known about the sale at least a week before Linville told Barbara Jean.

Interesting, but what was the significance?

"Mr. Bynum wanted photocopies of everything," said the clerk. "Want me to make you a copy, too?"

I thanked her but declined the offer. No point duplicating what I already had. And it looked like I'd have a nice quiet weekend to finish reading the rest of the stack.

I commandeered an unoccupied phone and left a message on Aunt Zell's machine as to why I wouldn't be home that weekend. I've had my own set of rooms in Aunt Zell and Uncle Ash's house since Mother died; and although I come and go freely, I do try to let her know my general plans. It tickles me that a childless, unemployed woman nearing seventy is so actively in her world that she needs an answering machine.

Next I called Social Services and got through to the Shelby Spivey Chet had mentioned. She sighed when I told her who I was and why I was calling.

"I know it probably seems bad to you, Judge Knott, but we *are* monitoring that situation. I did the initial field investigation on that child myself, and if it'll make you feel any better, I do believe that his grandfather really loves him. Most of the time, he's patient. He's teaching him how to fish and build boats, the boy does attend school and all his physical needs are being met."

She sighed again in my ear. "There doesn't seem to be any systematic violence, but according to the neighbors, Mr. Davis does lose it about three or four times a year and then he hauls off and smacks whoever's closest that can't hit back. The trouble is, the child's old enough now to testify, but he won't. And neither will his grandmother, so our hands are pretty much tied. Unless you'd be willing to attest that you've witnessed incidents of abuse yourself?"

I had to admit that I hadn't. All I had were suspicions.

We agreed that it was a hell of a way to protect our young.

"They keep making the stretch size of net mesh bigger and bigger to save the little game fish," she said unexpectedly. "Wish they'd take another look at the size of *our* mesh."

CHAPTER 10

I tell you, wife, it did me good
To sing that hymn once more;
I felt like some wrecked mariner
Who gets a glimpse of shore.
I almost want to lay aside
This weather-beaten form,
And anchor in the blessed port,
Forever from the storm.

—*John H. Yates*

As long as I was taking care of business with the deeds office and Social Services, I stopped by the Sheriff's Department and asked for Detective Smith. I wanted to tell him about Andy Bynum's files, but I wasn't any luckier there. The clerk on duty said she reckoned he ought to be back by two, though she wasn't real sure, which left me at loose ends.

When I drove in that morning, large ragged patches of blue had begun to show through. Now, as I retrieved my car from beneath the courthouse live oaks at a little before one, the gray clouds had all turned white and they sailed clean and fresh against pure cerulean.

Ignoring the promises I'd made to my wounded face at dawn, I gingerly smoothed another layer of makeup over the scratches, dug a pair of oversized Jackie O. sunglasses out of my glove compartment, and drove down to Front Street. Might as well take F. Roger Longmire's relayed blessing and enjoy Beaufort. There was a whole complex of shops right on the water that I hadn't visited this trip, so I parked there and went inside.

From the luscious aroma that met me at the entrance, I could tell that the Fudge Factory was still doing business, but I resisted. At least, I resisted till I'd finished browsing in the Rocking Chair Book Store, where I picked up Glenn Lawson's book on how the Army Corps of Engineers cooperates with business and agri-industries to despoil our wetlands (I wanted to see some facts and figures on the broader environmental issues), an ecological field guide to seacoast biota, and—in case the weekend dragged—a paperback mystery. Then, savoring a tiny square of still-warm fudge, I strolled along the boardwalk. At one point, I thought I saw Chet Winberry out of the corner of my eye, but when I looked back, whoever it was must have stepped into one of the shops.

Oddly enough, I did see someone I recognized. Zeke Myers, the stocky man who'd been so furious with Linville Pope about the boat she sold him, was leaning with his back against the railing and a dour expression on his face.

Pennants snapped in the wind, the smell of fried fish mingled with salt water, and knots of vacationers lingered along the walk to compare boats. I wasn't sure if I was glad or disappointed when I realized that the *Rainmaker* was no longer among the gleaming craft tied up there. Part of me was miffed that Lev hadn't called again, hadn't turned up in my courtroom to apologize, hadn't tried to move the moon and stars to lure me to his bed again before he left—not that it would have done him any good, of course.

("Oh yeah?")

The other part . . . well, the other part was academic, I told myself, since by now the *Rainmaker* was probably somewhere on a canal in the middle of the Great Dismal Swamp.

The parking lot was nearly full as I threaded my way around cars to stick the books in my trunk. A gentle tap of a horn made me look around.

"Hey, Deborah!" It was Linville Pope in a black convertible that I instantly coveted, sleek and sporty, with butterscotch leather interior. For me, I was probably looking at a whole year's salary. For Linville, probably one commission on a sale.

She slowed to a crawl. "You are not by any miracle leaving, are you?"

"Sorry," I said, slamming closed the trunk lid of my suddenly dowdy-looking car.

"Listen, if you are going to be around later, why not stop by my house for a quiet drink? Say five-ish?"

Without hesitating, I said, "Thanks, I'd love to." I didn't know what her ulterior motive was for asking, but I figured it might give me clues to whether Barbara Jean's accusations had validity and whether Linville was the one I chased last night.

Cars had begun to pile up behind her, so Linville gave me a wave and kept moving.

The *Rainmaker*'s departure meant I no longer had to avoid the waterfront, and the deck at the Ritchie House looked so inviting with its pink umbrellas and white chairs and tables that I decided to have a late lunch there.

The main lunch crowd had departed, but half the tables were still filled with boat loungers who lingered over coffee or early drinks.

They are a class unto themselves, these rootless wanderers who have cut their ties to land and live year-round on the water, moving like schools of restless fish up and down the Intracoastal Waterway. Sit in any waterfront restaurant or lounge and you'll see them drifting south in the fall, heading north in the spring. From huge sailing yachts to modest houseboats, they idle in on the changing tides, seldom straying further than a short stroll from the docks. The men in turtlenecks and gold-trimmed captain's hats, the women suntanned and vivid in silk scarves and tailored slacks, like calls to like. They pull several tables together in saltwater camaraderie and speak of "the Vineyard," Saint Croix, Hilton Head. Often they're not quite sure whether they're in North or South Carolina. The towns, the bars, the marinas must blend together over the years.

They remind me of migratory birds and I was bemused by their chatter and pleased when the waiter seated me near the railing where I could watch their coming and going. As I peered around the edge of the menu, I was startled to see Mrs. Docksider, Lev's partner's wife, heading across the deck toward me.

Did this mean that the *Rainmaker* was only out cruising around the sound?

"Judge Knott." She was very thin and conveyed such porcelain fragility that I was surprised by her deep voice and strong Boston accent. "I'm Catherine Llewellyn, Lev Schuster's partner."

Automatically, I took the hand she offered. "Partner?" It wasn't the first time I deserved a swift kick for making the same assumptions a lot of men do.

She looked puzzled. "Lev didn't tell you one of his partners was traveling with him?"

"For some reason, I thought he meant your husband. Sorry. If it's about my judgment Tuesday—?"

"No, no," she assured me. "You had no other option under the circumstances, but my sister was so sure she could convince a judge that I couldn't talk her out of agreeing to testify."

Either I've got to start working on my poker face or she's extraordinarily intuitive because even though I was wearing three layers of makeup and dark glasses, Catherine Llewellyn caught my skepticism.

"Claire only needs the puppet when there are strangers, Judge Knott." She glanced at my table and saw that it was set for only one person. "You're lunching alone?"

"Yes."

"Would it be an awful imposition if I joined you?" Her husky voice was urgent.

Curious, I gestured toward the opposite chair. "Please do."

When the waiter returned, I ordered black bean soup and half a club sandwich; Mrs. Llewellyn opted for the crab-stuffed tomato plate.

The breeze off Taylors Creek was warm and barely ballooned the pink canvas umbrella above us, but she drew a wisp of red silk from her pocket and tied it so her hair wouldn't blow. As we waited to be served, she spoke of the charms of Beaufort, the beauty of the Carolina coast, the friendliness of the people, the four-star comforts of the Ritchie House and the pleasures of a rare vacation. Then she asked me to call her Catherine and kept tagging so many Judge Knotts onto every sentence that I finally surrendered just as our food arrived.

"Please. Call me Deborah."

"Deborah." She turned my name in her mind and smiled appreciatively. "How very apt. Did your parents expect you to be a judge from birth?"

"Hardly." Not with a father who had only grudgingly agreed to help pay for law school and who had been quite negative about my decision to run for district judge.

She had been covertly studying me ever since we sat down, yet it was as if she didn't see my cuts and scratches because she was looking even deeper. "Deborah, may we speak frankly?"

That smokey voice, that prim Boston accent—I bet she did okay in the courtroom.

"I've wondered a lot about you these past few years. I hope you won't resent that?"

I stiffened. "Resent that you wondered, or resent what you're going to ask?"

She reached into her tote bag and drew out a lumpy envelope. "I believe these are yours?"

Inside were a dozen or more crystal beads. They flashed and sparkled against the stiff yellow paper like the prismed promises of the Crystal Coast.

"They were on the *Rainmaker* yesterday morning. Lev wasn't sure if you'd want them back."

Her indulgent smile invited me to share female solidarity over male obtuseness. I dug up a smile of my own and pasted it on my lips.

"Thanks."

The tines of her fork toyed with the crabmeat. "I'm not trying to pry, Deborah. It's just that I'm very fond of Lev. He's like the brother I never had and I don't want to see him hurt."

"You don't have to worry about that from me," I assured her.

"No? You were together how long? A year? A year and a half?"

"Something like that."

"Did you know you were the first?"

"That he'd lived with? Yes."

"And the last."

I almost dropped my soup spoon. "You're kidding!"

She shook her head. "Oh, I'm not saying there haven't been *women*. A couple of times there I even thought . . . but they always turn out to be unsuitable and he just can't seem to commit again to a long-term relationship."

I was appalled. Then flattered. Then baffled. If we were all that wonderful together, how come we were apart?

Apparently, Catherine Llewellyn wondered, too.

Determinedly, I changed the subject. "Lev tells me y'all have a divorce practice."

She was willing to wait. "Divorce and marital, yes. There are four partners and two associates: two men, four women."

"You seem to be doing all right. Lev told me that the *Rainmaker* was part of a fee."

"Ah, that was fun. The wife was a medical secretary, who put him through med school, struggled beside him through the early years and then, once the practice was generating big bucks, he bought the boat he had yearned for all his life—custom fitted to his specifications."

"His dream boat?" I murmured.

"Precisely. Right down to the sexy little first mate to swab the deck in a bikini. When the split came, we could have vacuumed his ass-sets, but she was willing to be equitable about it so long as she got the boat. Which she signed over to us almost immediately in lieu of fees since most of the settlement was in real property."

I was amused by the zest she seemed to take in that element of revenge. "Do you always represent the wife?"

"Not always. And sometimes we go in as *amicus curiae* on behalf of the children involved. In a way, child advocacy is part of the reason we've come to Beaufort."

"Another *amicus* case?"

"Not exactly." She snapped a piece of melba toast in half and put a dab of crab salad on it. "Perhaps I should fill in some personal background because that's where it began." She hesitated, choosing her words as carefully as she chose a speck of tomato to add to the salad.

"Claire's crazy about Lev, of course."

"Oh?" I said neutrally.

"He's like an uncle both to my son and to Claire."

Having only a couple of elderly aunts himself, Lev always did envy my large, and at times smothering, family. But Uncle Levvie?

"As you've seen, my sister's much younger than I. My father died, and Claire was by our mother's second husband. He was a wonderful father, but not much of a husband, so when Claire was four, there was a bitter divorce and custody fight, which Mother won. The man our mother next married—" Catherine Llewellyn's husky voice stumbled. "I'll blame myself till the day I die even though I was already married myself and studying law and there's no way I could have known. Claire blamed herself, you see, for her own father's disappearance in her life; and she thought she deserved it when that—that—*slime*—"

She took a deep breath. "By the time Jonathan and I realized, the damage was done. We took her to live with us, but my bright and bubbly, innocent little sister had withdrawn into borderline schizophrenia. When Lev came into our lives, he was gentle and perceptive. She had an old hand puppet—a kitten—and Lev talked to the kitten, not to her. The first time the kitten answered him, I wept. He brought a half-dozen more puppets the next time he came and Claire seized on the blonde-haired doll like a lifeline back to reality. I know Tuesday may have seemed ridiculous to you, but if you could only know what a giant step it represented for Claire."

"Then I really am sorry I had to rule against her."

"Actually, Lev thinks it might be better in the long run. Reinforces the idea that she must begin to speak for herself."

It was a sad story, but I didn't see how it related to their being in Beaufort.

"Since we began practice, we've seen the trauma that divorce can wreak on children's lives. Wealth cannot automatically insulate a child from the guilt and angst when a family breaks apart. Indeed, wealth often exacerbates the situation."

She seemed to hear her words and smiled sheepishly. "Sorry. I get didactic on the subject. Anyhow, to put it simply, we have some funds and we hope to create a center for kids who're involved in messy divorces and custody fights, a safe and interesting place where they can talk out their fears with children who're in a similar situation, and get the counseling and decompression that they need to survive while their parents—and, yes, their parents' attorneys—battle it out.

"North Carolina gives very good tax incentives to locate here and Beaufort itself meets a lot of our criteria. The climate's moderate, the water's clean. The library's adequate, the marine museum has good programs for youth, there's a hospital in Morehead. Overall, Beaufort's small enough, safe enough, and still cheap enough that we think we can create something quite special if we can find some commercial waterfront property within walking or bicycling distance of downtown."

"Ah," I said, as the light broke. "Neville Fishery."

"Precisely. Land-use regulations make it simpler if we convert a commercial property already in existence than if we tried to get the permits to build new from scratch on undeveloped property."

Curious, I asked, "Those funds you mentioned. Are they like a grant or from private backers?"

"Oh, it would be an investment opportunity," she acknowledged.

("So they'll cleanse wealthy parents of their own guilt and angst and turn a neat profit, too," said the pragmatist, busily punching figures into his calculator. *"Lev baby really has come a long way from pasta and walk-ups.")*

("Would you visit the parents' iniquity upon their young?" chided the preacher. *"Surely even the rich are entitled to cushion their children from hurts.")*

("That's what I mean. And hey, betcha the Rainmaker *gets to be a business deduction before it's all over.")*

"Lev says you're a friend of Neville Fishery's owner," Catherine Llewellyn said. "Tell me, do you think a personal appeal would help? If we explained to her what we planned for the site?"

"I really doubt it," I said honestly. "But who knows? Her husband would like it if she'd sell, but there's been so much rancor and controversy over the future of the menhaden industry that she may well dig in her heels and tough it out. Aren't there other properties?"

"None quite like this one," she said regretfully.

At the next table over, a paunchy guy with Grecian Formula hair beneath his captain's hat spread a chart across the table and began to give a lesson in navigation to a bubbly young thing half his age.

The waiter tried to interest us in his dessert card, but we both turned him down. Nor would I let Catherine get my check.

"Nevertheless, it's good we had this chance to meet, Deborah," she said, with a gracious incline of her porcelain head. "I feel it's helped me know Lev even better somehow."

"I'm so glad," I murmured. My mother taught me a few graces, too.

⌘

When I slid under the steering wheel of my car a few minutes later, I was dismayed to see the backseat half down and the contents of my trunk exposed. More than one of my brothers had lectured me on this possibility. "What's the point of locking things in your trunk if you don't lock the car itself?" they'd ask.

I got out and unlocked the trunk button to survey the damage.

Oddly, nothing was missing. Oh, it had obviously been tossed—my new books were now half under the tarp I keep there, my garment bag had a tiny bit of my black judge's robe caught in the zipper—but my .38 was still locked in the tool box, and my briefcase hadn't been taken.

Weird. Unless . . .?

A young man was perched on a nearby railing and I was in the middle of asking if he'd noticed anyone plundering my car, when I realized he was Jay Hadley's son, Josh.

"Yeah, I thought I'd seen you before," he said, his dark eyes darting away from mine. "They take anything?"

"Not that I can tell. But you didn't notice anyone?"

He slipped down from his perch. "I was just waiting for my sister and yonder she comes."

Before I could question him further, he'd threaded his way across the busy street and jumped into a pickup driven by his sister.

If Zeke Myers had still been around, I'd have asked him, but that stocky little man had vanished. And if Linville Pope had found a parking space in this parking lot, she had finished her business quickly and gone because her sleek black convertible was nowhere in sight either.

Was it possible someone knew I had Andy Bynum's papers?

I found a pay phone, called Jay Hadley and, after swearing her to secrecy, told her that Andy's desk had been ransacked last night, and my car searched today. "Who knows you gave me those files?" I asked.

"I may have mentioned it to some of the Alliance members that were at the funeral yesterday," she admitted.

She rattled off a bunch of names, but the only ones I recognized were Telford Hudpeth and Barbara Jean Winberry and I rather doubted if either of them wanted to keep me from discovering any of Linville Pope's possibly shady dealings.

As I returned to my car, something drew my attention to an upper balcony of the Ritchie House. There, lounging in a white wicker rocker, Claire Montgomery stared down at me. As our eyes met, the flaxen-haired hand puppet came up in an unmistakable gesture.

Damned if it didn't give me the finger.

I resisted the impulse to reply in kind—conduct unbecoming, etc. Instead, since it was now almost three o'clock, I tried Quig Smith's office again.

"Sorry, Judge," said the uniformed duty officer. "He was in, but now he's gone again. Want me to have him call you when he checks in next?"

"No," I decided. "I'll stop by one more time before I leave Beaufort."

Back on Front Street, I bought a floppy straw hat, sandals, and a pair of shorts and had the clerk bag up my skirt along with my heels and panty-hose. I also borrowed their restroom to remove every smidgen of makeup. The soap stung the scratches on my cheek and forehead, yet it seemed to me that some of the redness was beginning to fade from the edges. With sunglasses and hat in place, it was moot anyhow.

Five minutes later, I was driving across the causeway, through Morehead City and across another bridge to Atlantic Beach, where I took a left onto 58 and continued on to Fort Macon, now a state park.

The original colonial forts washed into the sea in the early 1800s and the current one of heavy masonry was built in the 1830s. Periodically, the fort is threatened by the sea, and statewide debates rage in the newspapers as to whether or not herculean methods should be used to save it. As far as I'm concerned, the sea giveth and the sea can taketh away. But then I've always been personally outraged by people who build their play places—retirement or vacation houses—on narrow sandbars and then expect the rest of us to pay higher taxes and higher insurance rates so that they can rebuild when the inevitable storms wipe the beaches clean again. If they want to take the risk, fine, but leave me out of it. And that goes for old forts, too.

Still, as long as it's here, Fort Macon's an interesting place to tour. I stood on the ramparts and gazed out to sea. If I didn't look back at all the piers and high rises straggling down the sandy stretches, I could almost imagine what it must have been like to guard this point two hundred years ago against Spanish and British raiders.

Then a jet ski roared past, breaking the illusion.

I slipped off my sandals and strolled briskly along the wide beach, occasionally wetting my toes in the cool water, my mind blanked except for the rolling waves, the gleam of colored shells, the grace of sandpipers that ran across the clean white sand and left lines of tiny neat tracks like featherstitching on a crazy quilt.

There were very few people walking here since the surf wasn't yet warm enough for swimming. The sandpipers and I had it mostly to ourselves.

At the water's edge, I found a couple of hermit crabs, one in a lettered olive shell, the other in a moon snail shell, and suddenly remembered how my younger cousin Scotty used to love to race them. Feeling thirteen again, I drew a three-foot circle in the wet sand, placed both crabs in the exact middle and even let the bigger one be Scott's.

At once, it all rushed back: how patiently we squatted down by the circle to wait till the crabs emerged: one cautious claw, then another, then a skittering run for the sea. My crab was smaller but less cautious than Scott's and soon it began its rush for safety. Scott's emerged, oriented itself, and scuttled after mine, and I could hear Scotty's adolescent sports announcer voice in my ear like the ocean in a conch shell:

"And it's Lettered Olive coming down the home stretch and here comes Moon Snail moving up on the outside. Lettered Olive is digging in and Moon Snail pulls to the right. Moon Snail making his move now. Lettered Olive holding on. Moon Snail jockeying for position and at the line—YES! It's Lettered Olive by half a shell! And the crowd goes wild, folks, as both crabs tumble into the waves. Yea-aa-aa!"

I stood up and brushed sand from my knees as Scott's boyish voice faded.

And now he was a father himself and by next summer, he would be racing hermit crabs with baby Arlie and the cycle would begin all over again.

It was a lovely peaceful hour and not until I turned back toward the car was I reclaimed by the muddle of Lev and Catherine Llewellyn, Barbara Jean and her menhaden factory, Mahlon Davis and his seething resentments, young Guthrie, Jay Hadley, Linville Pope and her machinations, and over all, Andy Bynum's murder and the push/pull feuding over water usage. The only unadulterated bright spot in the whole mess was Kidd Chapin and he was the only one I couldn't count on seeing again.

When I reached the car, I slipped my beige-and-turquoise skirt back on and slid off my shorts. At the bathhouse, I rinsed the sand off my feet and put on my new sandals. A splash of cool water on my face, a light cover of makeup, and I was ready to drop by for that "quiet drink" at Linville Pope's.

⌘

My watch said it was a suitably five-ish 5:10 when I rang the doorbell at Linville Pope's house.

The man who opened the door was a physical wreck: barefooted, stained khakis, lank-haired and gaunt-faced. He reeked of bourbon and he held out a cordless phone that was smeared with blood.

"Can't make thish damn thing work," he sobbed drunkenly. "Call them."

"Call who?" I asked, shrinking back from the gory object.

"P'leesh. Somebody's killed my wife!"

CHAPTER 11

Whether the wrath of the storm-tossed sea,
Or demons, or men, or whatever it be,
No water can swallow the ship where lies
The Master of ocean and earth and skies;
They all shall sweetly obey My will;
Peace, be still! Peace be still!
They all shall sweetly obey My will;
Peace, peace, be still!

—Mary A. Baker

Clasping the bloody phone to his chest, Midge Pope slowly slumped to the floor, moaning over and over, "Linvie, Linvie."

I stepped over his outstretched legs and moved cautiously through the house.

No one in the public rooms, no one in the kitchen.

At the end of a curiously austere hall, I heard a low radio and when I pushed the door open, I saw a muscular young man, fully dressed, stretched out on a double bed, sound asleep. The radio beside him was tuned to easy rock.

"Hello?"

His eyes blinked open when I spoke and he stared at me blankly for a moment, then jumped up guiltily.

"Oh Jeez!" he said, "I must have dropped off. You won't tell her, will you? I—"

An open door connected to the next room and he glanced inside and groaned, "He's gone! She's gonna kill me!"

He turned and almost slammed into me. "Sorry, but I've got to find him and—"

"Try the front door," I suggested.

It was clear to me that he'd been hired to baby-sit Linville Pope's alcoholic husband and that he was so shook at losing his charge, I'd get nothing out of him till he'd found Midge Pope again.

"Where's Mrs. Pope?" I asked as he rushed across the entry hall to help Pope to his feet.

"Down at the landing, probably. She said she was—"

At that moment, he saw both the telephone and Pope's bloody hands. "Oh Jeez!"

I didn't wait to hear more. Already I was running through the wide sunroom. The locked French doors hindered me a moment, but once I was through them, I raced across the wide terrace, over the grass, and out to the landing.

Linville Pope's crumpled figure lay near the end of the long planked dock. She was still wearing the black-and-white checked shirt and full black skirt she'd had on when I saw her earlier. She'd fallen backward and strands of ash-blond hair half-hid her face. I knelt to touch the pulse points in her neck and wrists.

Nothing. Already the living warmth had drained from her skin.

It was too much like finding Andy Bynum—the swirling hair, the bright red stain that blossomed through her shirt, the lifeless pallor. At least her eyes were closed. Numbed though I was, somehow I found myself thinking how much bigger she looked lying there dead than she had when erect and full of life.

For a long moment, her death filled every interstice of awareness un-til finally, as if from a far distance, the sound of an outboard motor penetrated my ears and I turned to see a small dinghy headed for a boat moored a few hundred feet out in the channel.

The *Rainmaker.*

Benumbed, I watched Lev Schuster secure a line and pull himself aboard. He glanced back and seemed to hesitate upon seeing me there on the dock. At this distance, I wasn't sure if he could recognize me; but whether or not he did, he quickly disappeared below. At the moment there seemed to be no other boats in the immediate vicinity, but I suppose the expanse of marshy hummocks that lay between Lennox Point and Harkers Island could have concealed whole fleets of small skiffs or dories.

Footsteps thudded down the dock behind me. Midge Pope's baby-sitter.

"Is she—?"

"Go back," I said sharply. "It's too late to help her. Just stay there at the end and don't let anyone out here. I'm going to call the police."

He was too young to argue with me and I hurried past and into the sunroom where I remembered seeing a phone during the party on Tuesday.

I got through to Quig Smith almost immediately.

"Hey there!" he said jovially. "Our desk officer bet me I'd be gone 'fore you called again. You're just lucky my new ecology journal that came in today had an article on estuarine pollution and fish nurseries or I'd be—"

I cut through and he listened in silence to what I had to say. When I'd finished, he said, "How 'bout you make sure the door's unlocked so we can get in, then go on back out and keep a watch. I'll be there in ten minutes."

Out in the hallway, Midge Pope had blacked out and was lying curled in a fetal position around the cordless phone. No need to shift him since he was no longer blocking the entrance. I left the door on the latch and hurried back down to the dock, where the young man stood with a sick expression on his face.

"Not much longer," I told him. "I'm Deborah Knott, and you're—"

"Simon McGuire. What happened here, ma'am?"

"Don't *you* know?"

"No, ma'am," he said, shaking a thatch of reddish-brown hair that was still rumpled from his stolen nap. "She said some judge was coming and for me to keep Midge—Mr. Pope—in his room. I finally got him to bed and I just lay down to rest a couple of minutes myself and the next thing I knew, there you were."

He had a pronounced lantern jaw, square shoulders, and a dazed expression on his open face. In his jeans and sneakers, he looked no more than twenty or twenty-one and could be any student from East Carolina or Carteret Community College.

Before I could ask him when he'd last seen Linville alive, I saw that Lev was back in his dinghy and heading straight across the water toward us.

"Stay here," I told McGuire and went down to the end of the pier.

As Lev cut the motor of his dinghy and readied a line to tie up, I called, "Stay back. Linville Pope's been shot."

"I know." He looped the line around a post. "I found her."

"You might be destroying evidence."

"I told you—I tied up here ten minutes ago. This won't make any difference."

He secured the boat and stepped up onto the dock. "I called nine-one-one and they're sending someone."

"Called?"

"Cellular phone on the boat," he explained.

"Why didn't you call from the house?"

"The doors were locked and I thought it'd be quicker to call from the boat than try to hunt up the neighbors. God, this is awful! That poor woman." He moved restlessly from one side of the dock to the other.

I'd forgotten what a pacer Lev was. Whenever something upset him, whenever he was working out the elements of a complex case—it's as if his brain can't function under stress without his legs moving. He paced now, back and forth, with that old familiar urgency.

I drew back at the sight of a blood smear on his khakis and said, "Who shot her, Lev?"

He followed my eyes and brushed at the smear. "When I tried to get a pulse, I must have—" He gave me a sharp look, then in a level voice said, "I don't know, Red. She was like that when I got here just a few minutes ago."

I was puzzled as to why he'd even be here since Linville had invited me and she hadn't struck me as someone who invited confrontations. "Was she expecting you?"

"Not really. She marked some places on my chart along the straits back to Harkers Island for me to look at today." He gestured vaguely across the marshes toward the east. "I was on my way back to Beaufort, and thought I'd swing by here to ask if she could show me one of the properties tomorrow. When I first saw her—"

His eyes were snagged by movement behind me. I turned and saw Quig Smith striding across the terrace, accompanied by another detective and a couple of uniformed Carteret County sheriff's deputies.

"That was quick," said Lev.

I glanced at my watch. Smith had said ten minutes.

It had only been eight.

⌘

The rescue squad, summoned by Lev's 911 call, arrived almost immediately after Smith and his men and had, at first, mistaken Midge Pope for the victim since they thought the blood on his shirt came from his body when they found him curled in the entry hall.

Now it was déjà vu time.

Watching the two teams out on the dock was uncannily like last Sunday afternoon when I'd watched these same people go through the same motions around Andy Bynum's body. Only, instead of rocking in a boat to answer Quig Smith's questions, this time we sat around a table on Linville Pope's terrace as we each gave our accounts of the afternoon.

The base of the table was three bronze dolphins that had weathered to a soft green; the top was a thick round slab of glass with dozens of seashells embedded just below the surface. I recognized sand dollars, scotch bonnets, tulips, tritons, olives and snails. It seemed unreal that only an hour before I'd been happily racing hermit crabs in similar shells and now I was back in the middle of another murder.

Smith questioned me first, then Simon McGuire. I was not surprised to hear that the young man was indeed between semesters. After two years at Cullowhee up in the mountains, he was taking a year off at the beach to earn more tuition money while trying to figure out what he really wanted to be when he grew up. Linville had hired him only two weeks ago when Midge Pope checked himself out of a sanitarium up near Asheville and came back to Beaufort to start drinking again.

"My girlfriend's mother is office manager for Mrs. Pope and she knew I had experience working as a hospital orderly for a couple of summers, so when Mrs. Pope said she was looking for somebody right away, Mrs. Abbott told her about me."

On his first day there, he told us, Midge Pope was present when Linville Pope outlined his duties.

"She told him she wasn't going to try to keep him from drinking anymore. If he was determined to kill himself, she knew she couldn't stop it, but she couldn't watch and she couldn't be with him every minute. She said if he'd agree to let me help him so he didn't drive drunk or get out on a boat drunk or walk in the road where somebody might run over him, then she'd see that there was a case of bourbon in his sitting room from here on out."

She was half-crying when she said it, McGuire told us. And Midge had taken her hands and there were tears in his own eyes when he told her how very sorry he was that he was such a poor excuse for a husband. "She said she'd rather have him like he was than any other man in Beaufort and then they went off together to her rooms down at the other end of the house and I thought maybe they weren't going to need me after all," said McGuire. "But by that evening, Midge was blind out of his mind drunk and I swear I don't think he's been cold stone sober fifteen minutes since then."

Hardly more than a boy, Simon McGuire seemed thoroughly shaken by Linville's death, and as it all sank in, he was now ravaged by guilt. "If I wasn't asleep," he castigated himself, "I might have—"

"I doubt it," Smith said kindly. "It'd be nice if you'd been a witness so you could describe who shot her, but hell, son, you might've been shot then, too. Who knows? Now when did you actually last see Miz Pope?"

"Between three-thirty and four," he hazarded. "She came into Midge's sitting room to say she'd asked some judge to come by for a drink about five—" He looked around as if expecting a black-robed figure to suddenly come strolling through the French doors.

"That was me," I told him.

"You're a judge?"

Under different circumstances, I might have been nettled by his excessive surprise. Now I let it pass with a nod.

"Anyhow," he continued, "she said she was going to go check on the boat—she just bought a new little runabout—and then freshen up. When she was expecting company, I was supposed to keep Midge in his wing of the house. That was another part of their bargain, but today he was sort of ornery about it and wouldn't settle down. I thought he'd finally passed out but for some reason he must've got out while I was asleep and then Miss—the Judge woke me up."

His long square jaw tightened convulsively and Smith patted his shoulder.

As Smith turned in his chair, Lev sat back warily.

"And you, Mr. Schuster?"

Again, Lev explained about spending the afternoon cruising around back of Harkers Island looking at various pieces of property and then his decision to drop in on Linville.

"You happen to notice any other boats around as you turned into the channel?" asked Smith.

"I wasn't paying too much attention," Lev admitted. "According to the chart, when you swing around the point here, the channel goes from seventeen feet of water to seven quite rapidly and if you don't keep your eyes on the channel markers, you can run aground because it's only two or three feet deep on either side."

Quig Smith nodded. "All the same, Mr. Schuster, weren't there any other boats in the channel?"

Beneath the deep ledges of his brow, Lev's eyes narrowed as he tried to remember. "As I started my turn, there was a speedboat going straight in to Taylors Creek, back toward Beaufort. I guess I noticed because it's a no-wake zone and the guy hadn't cut his speed yet. Once I got around on this side though, the channel ends just a few hundred feet on and there was nothing as big as me there." Absently, he twisted a tuft of his short beard as he concentrated. "I think I might have passed some small open boats when I skirted the marshes, but I was concentrating so hard on the channel I couldn't begin to say for sure."

"So you moored out there in the channel about when, would you say?"

"About a quarter to five," Lev answered promptly. "I remember thinking it wasn't quite time to splice the mainbrace but that maybe Mrs. Pope would offer me a beer anyhow. I got the dinghy into the water and as I motored over, I saw something white and black lying on the pier, but it wasn't till I got out of the dinghy that I realized it was her. I thought maybe she'd fallen or something and then I saw all the blood and couldn't get a pulse. I ran up to the house, but the doors were locked and nobody came when I pounded on them, so I ran back down and took the dinghy back to my boat because I had a cellular—"

His voice faltered and we all became aware that Midge Pope had appeared in the doorway. His bloody shirt was half off, he now wore thonged sandals on his sockless feet, his hair was damp as if he'd held it under a stream of cold water and he looked ghastly. But though his hand held a half-empty bottle of Early Times and though his hand shook as he pointed it at Lev, his voice was strong when he roared, "You Jew bastard! You killed my wife!"

"Hey, now, Midge," said Smith, grabbing Pope before he could swing that bottle at Lev.

"He did, Quig. I saw him. I was standing right at those windows and I saw him. Bastard sat right out there in his boat and took aim at Linvie with his rifle and dropped her like a beautiful loon. You know how beautiful they are, Quig?"

"I know, Midge. I know."

"I told Linvie, I said, 'Honey, you look cuter'n a loon today in your black-and-white checked feathers,' and she laughed and time I got to her, she was gone, Quig. Gone."

Rage dissipated into grief.

"What'd you do then, Midge?" Smith asked gently.

"Tried to call you, but the damn phone wouldn't work," he sobbed. "And he followed me up to the house, but I saw him coming," he said with drunken craftiness, "and I locked the doors so he couldn't get in, but the phone . . ."

156

He pulled away from Smith and shambled toward the dock.

"Aw now, Midge, you don't want to go out there," said Smith. "How 'bout you let ol' Simon here take you inside and get slicked up first? Linville wouldn't want people to see you looking like this, now would she?"

McGuire sprang up and Midge Pope allowed himself to be led away.

Silence enveloped the terrace.

"Now just a damn minute here," said Lev. "You're not going to believe an anti-Semitic alkie that hasn't drawn a sober breath in two weeks, are you? Red?"

Smith raised his eyebrows at that. Until then, he hadn't realized that we knew each other, but he didn't let that deter him. "No, sir, I'm not saying I do; but just because Midge is drunk don't mean he can't see. You admit that you followed him here to the house."

"No, I do *not* admit that. When I pulled in at the dock, I did not see anybody except Mrs. Pope lying there alone. I'm not saying he didn't go out and touch her, not with all that blood on his clothes, but he sure as hell wasn't there when I got here. How do you know he wasn't the one who shot her and then went out to check that she was dead?"

"Yes, that's a possibility," Smith admitted, "and that's why I'm going to ask Judge Knott here if she'll sign a probable cause warrant for me to search this house for a recently fired gun, even though it could be lying off the end of the dock out there in the mud somewhere for all I know."

I nodded mutely and he summoned one of the uniformed deputies to go out to the car and get him a couple of search warrant forms.

"I don't want you to take this the wrong way, Mr. Schuster, but I'm gonna ask to search your boat, too."

"You don't need a warrant, Detective Smith," Lev said hotly. "I'll waive my Fourth Amendment rights and you can go take a look right now."

"Lev," I said warningly.

"I've got nothing to hide, Red."

"Well, now, if it's all the same to you and the Judge, I'd just as soon do it by the book," said Smith.

"I quite agree," I said crisply.

In the ensuing awkward silence, Lev suddenly seemed to notice the scratches beneath my makeup. "You hurt yourself."

"It's nothing. I wasn't watching where I was going," I said, but my injuries reminded me that I'd wanted to tell Quig Smith about Andy Bynum's papers. This wasn't the time or place though.

The officer returned with the forms and Smith filled them out in scrupulous detail, affirming that the only object he would search for would be a recently fired shoulder weapon. "'Cause Midge does know guns," he told me, "but at that distance, it could've been a single-barreled shotgun or a rifle."

He passed the forms over to me and I signed and dated them both.

"You mind if one of my men uses your dinghy, Mr. Schuster?" Smith asked.

"You sure you don't want her to sign a form for that, too?"

"Well, now—"

"Oh, go ahead!" he said tightly.

Smith instructed his officers, then told me I could leave if I wanted.

"I'll wait," I said.

"Not on my account, I hope." Lev's voice was bitter.

"If you like, I can call Catherine Llewellyn to come," I offered.

"You honestly think I'm going to need professional counsel?"

"No, but you were the one who used to say anybody that represented himself had a fool for a client." I tried to make my tone light and I got a ghost of a smile beneath his beard.

"I didn't shoot her, Red."

"I know you didn't."

For the first time since Midge Pope had leveled that accusation, Lev seemed to relax. "For a minute there—"

The rest of his words were drowned out as a helicopter suddenly appeared from nowhere and hovered over the pier where Linville's body was being loaded onto a gurney. It bore the logo of a Raleigh television station and must have been filming another story in the area to have arrived so quickly. Smith's men tried to wave it off, but it settled gently in a cleared space on the far side of the house and a cameraman quickly swept the whole area with his camcorder.

Soon as I realized what he was doing, I turned my face. All I'd need at this point was for my family back in Colleton County to see that I was involved in two separate murders down here in Carteret and I'd have to take my phone off the hook if I wanted to sleep tonight.

"We're going indoors," I called to Smith, but two seconds after we stepped inside I realized we'd avoided Scylla only to run afoul of Charybdis.

Local news reporters had arrived, along with cameramen from Greenville and New Bern. (We later learned a general had called a news conference to discuss whether or not Cherry Point would be affected by this newest wave of congressional base closings.) They swarmed through the open door as Linville's body was taken out to the ambulance, and strobe lights and microphones seemed to be everywhere. Fortunately, no one seemed to recognize me or to connect me with Andy Bynum's death. They were too interested in trying to get to Midge Pope or to get a statement from Quig Smith.

Simon McGuire had blocked access to Midge's wing and Smith was promising he'd take questions just as soon as he knew a little more himself.

The violent death of a woman this prominent was let's-go-live news in this area, of course, and if they hurried, they might even slide in a bulletin before the six o'clock report ended, so the first wave of questions was quick and dirty; and by the time they were ready for greater in-depth "details-at-eleven" interviews, Quig Smith had sent someone to escort us behind the yellow tape barrier.

The dinghy returned to the dock and the officer who'd searched the *Rainmaker* reported that he'd found no guns. Another had found Linville's gun case, but all the slots were filled and none of the weapons seemed to have been fired that day.

Smith announced we were both free to go and Lev said, "Come with me, Red? I can bring you back for your car after the feeding frenzy's over."

"Thanks, Lev, but I really think I'd rather run the gauntlet and go on back to Harkers Island."

He studied my face a long moment, then his own face cleared. With an air of relief (and surprise at that relief?), Lev gently touched the scratch on my cheek. "Take care of yourself, Red."

"You, too, kid."

Then he was gone and I tackled Smith myself. "Are these two murders connected?" I asked.

"I don't know," he told me candidly. "One thing though. No exit wound, so the bullet's probably still inside her. We should know by tomorrow night if it's the same gun or not."

While he was talking to the reporters, I managed to slip away with only minimum attention.

⌘

Linville's house was on the north side of the point, on North River; Chet and Barbara Jean were on the south side, on Taylors Creek; but their driveways were less than a quarter-mile apart, on opposite sides of Lennoxville Road.

Impulsively, I pulled into the Winberry drive, wound through the tall shrubs and live oaks that shielded them from public view and circled up to the front door.

"Deborah! What a nice surprise," said Barbara Jean when she answered the bell. There were tired circles under her eyes, but her smile was warm. "Chet said you were going home today."

"I was, but then Roger Longmire told 'em I could stay another week."

"Great. I just made a fresh pitcher of tea. Come on out to the porch and join me."

We went through the house to a sunny south-facing terrace that wasn't much smaller than Linville Pope's. Half of Barbara Jean's was covered, though; and where the porch roof ended, trellises of weathered cypress continued across the bricked terrace to provide filtered shade in the summertime.

"Oh, Lordy!" I breathed. The beauty was almost enough to ease the horror of finding Linville's body.

Barbara Jean's face lit up. "Don't you love this time of year?" she said.

Her azaleas had taken salty blasts from last month's bad storm and the leaves still showed large patches of brown although the white, pink and lavender blossoms gamely tried to cover; but her wisteria was drop-dead gorgeous. The thick ropy vines that covered the trellises were in full bloom and dripped with huge heavy clusters of purple blossoms that mingled with the cool salt air and late afternoon sunshine to fill the porch with a bewitching fragrance. Off to one side, an eclectic mixture of Adirondack and wicker chairs circled a wide low table and I sank down into one of them and breathed in deeply.

"How can you bear to go off to work every day and leave this?"

"Sometimes I don't," she confided. "I've been playing hooky all afternoon. Chet's off fishing somewhere so I borrowed a friend's runabout and got out on the water myself for an hour or two. I just needed some time alone for a change."

"I'm sorry I disturbed you then."

"No, no, I was ready for company."

I was overflowing about Linville but waited till she had poured me a glass of tea and assured herself that I had everything in the way of lemon, sugar, napkins, or cookies that a guest could want before I told her.

"Shot? On her own pier?"

She listened in total silence until I finished, then slowly shook her head. "Oh, shit, Deborah!" The embarrassed expression on her face was that of someone caught in a lapse of good taste. "God forgive me, you know what my first thought was?"

"That now that boat storage facility next to Jill won't be built?"

Barbara Jean gave a bleak smile. "I didn't know I could be this unchristian, this callous."

"It's not being callous. You guys weren't exactly best friends, she wanted Neville Fishery and she was threatening the peace and quiet of your daughter's home. It's only human to be relieved that those things will go on hold now."

She sighed and started asking for more details: when exactly did Quig Smith think she'd been killed? Had there been any witness?

"Midge? Midge was there?"

"Evidently he's been back a couple of weeks, holed up in his rooms, drinking steadily. He says he was standing in the sunroom and saw it happen. That someone out in a boat aimed a shoulder gun at Linville while she was down on the dock, but he was so drunk at the time, Smith's not sure he's a credible witness. I'm surprised you didn't hear the rescue truck's siren."

"No, I was—no, I didn't."

She set down her glass of iced tea and headed for the wet bar just inside the door. "I need something stiffer. Fix one for you?"

"No, thank you," I said, but I did stir an extra spoon of sugar into my tea.

When she returned, she carried an old-fashioned glass with two inches of something amber over a couple of ice cubes.

"Is that Chet coming in?" I asked, as a boat slowly peeled off from the channel.

We took our glasses and went down to meet him at the landing. As with most people who live on the water, he had cut his motor at the precise instant needed to lift it before the propeller blades scraped bottom, yet still had the momentum to carry him in to his dock.

Before he could even throw her a line, Barbara Jean began to tell him about Linville Pope's murder and made me finish.

"What?" Chet stood in the boat to listen before handing out a bucket of fish and getting out himself with a couple of rods. He was still walking stiffly from his pulled muscle and he shook his head. "My God, Deb'rah. You really stepped in the middle of it this week, didn't you, girl?"

Back at the house, he dumped the three fish he'd caught into a chest of ice—"Not much to show for a whole afternoon"—rinsed off his hands and took the drink Barbara Jean had fixed him.

"Poor Linville," he said. "And poor Midge. Half his problem is that he could never give her what she wanted."

"She wanted to be Queen of Beaufort," Barbara Jean said sharply. "Let's not forget that."

"De mortuis, honey."

"I'm *not* speaking ill of the dead," she argued. "Only the truth. She wanted to close Neville Fishery. She never knew what it was like before. No sense of history, no—"

She turned to me abruptly. "Did you ever hear them singing on the water, Deborah?"

"The chanteymen? No. I have one of the tapes though, and I can imagine how it must have sounded."

"You *can't!*" she said passionately, and I don't think it was the bourbon speaking. "When I was a little girl, we still had one boat that didn't have a power block, and my daddy used to let me go out with them once in a while. They'd let down the two little purse boats to circle a school of menhaden and the men had to pull the heavy nets by hand. That's why they sang those long slow chanties, to synchronize the hardening of the fish against the main boat. And the sound of those black voices floating across the water from one boat to the other—the leader would sing out the first words and the men would heave away as they echoed the strong slow beats—I'll never hear anything as beautiful again in my life."

Tears spilled from her eyes.

"Ah, honey," said Chet, taking her in his arms and patting her tenderly on the back.

"And that's what Linville Pope wanted to destroy."

"I thought the chanteymen were replaced by hydraulic net-pullers twenty years ago," I said, remembering how Linville had taunted her on that point. "She didn't have anything to do with that, did she?"

"But some of their sons still work for me. They link back into that heritage and continue the work their fathers did and she would have destroyed that link. And taken something precious from me as well."

She laid her head on Chet's shoulder. "I didn't wish Linville Pope dead, Deborah, but I can't say I'm sorry that I don't have to keep fighting her off."

I had to admit that given Linville's persistent techniques, there might well be a lot of similar feelings all around this part of Carteret County when the news got out.

Chet and Barbara Jean invited me to stay for supper, but it was getting too heavy for me.

"Sorry," I told them, "but I've got a bunch of reading to do and I'd better get to it."

"Andy's papers?" asked Barbara Jean.

"Papers?" said Chet.

"I told you about them this morning," she said. "That research Andy was doing on Pope Properties."

"Oh yeah. Find anything yet, Deborah?"

"Haven't had a chance. And I probably won't recognize it if it's there."

"Maybe you should let me take a look. I know most of the players. By name, anyhow, if not by person."

"If I don't spot anything tonight, maybe I will," I said.

"Why waste your time?" asked Barbara Jean. "Linville's dead now, remember? Nobody needs that ammunition anymore."

⌘

It was heading for twilight when I stopped at a store on the outskirts of town and picked up several sets of cheap underwear and two packages of panty-hose. If I was going to stay over another week, I'd have to find a laundromat, but not tomorrow, thank you. I planned to sleep in and then spend the day skimming through Andy Bynum's papers.

⌘

The smell of steamed shrimp hit my nose the instant I walked into the cottage. Indeed, I walked in through a door that was not only unlocked, but which could no longer be secured at all except by a padlock that I hadn't bothered with since I got to the island. Someone seemed to have put a foot against the door and shoved hard enough to tear the dead bolt right off the old brittle door casing.

"Good," said Kidd Chapin from somewhere in the dim interior. "You're back. I was beginning to think I'd have to spend the whole evening in darkness."

"So now the Wildlife Commission's into breaking and entering?"

"Believe it or not, it was like that when I got here about forty-five minutes ago. Everything was tossed, but you'll have to check it out to see what's missing. The TV's still here and the lock's intact on the pump house. This got anything to do with those files in your newspapers?"

"How the heck did you find them?" I asked, yanking down the shades so I could turn on the lights and see his expression when I threw him out.

He did have an embarrassed look on his thin homely face. "Well, when I came past and saw the lock was smashed, there was a bucket with some shrimp in it right by the door and you know you can't leave shrimp out too long. I couldn't head and shell them outside, so I grabbed up some of those newspapers and spread 'em over the table and out dropped a bunch of Xeroxes. You ever read *The Purloined Letter?*"

I had to laugh. "What did you do with the shrimp after you cleaned them?"

"I saved you some," he said virtuously. Then, in an abrupt change, he said, "I was in Quig's office when you called about the Pope woman. You okay?"

I nodded.

"Hey," he said gently. "Your face seems to be healing nicely." Then he took a closer look. "Better take the makeup off though and let it breathe."

Shaking my head, I went and changed into jeans, washed my face, put peroxide on my scratches, then called Telford Hudpeth and thanked him for the shrimp. "You didn't happen to notice anything about the front door here, did you?" I asked.

"No, ma'am. Why? Something wrong with it?"

"Someone broke in while I was gone. They didn't take anything, but I was just wondering if you saw them."

"Sure didn't, but all I did was set the bucket down and leave. If you don't have a way to lock your door, I can bring some tools and maybe scare up a new lock and—"

"That's okay," I said. "Thanks anyhow, but there's a padlock and a hasp I can still use."

"You're sure now?"

"I'm positive," I said firmly.

Kidd had blatantly eavesdropped on the whole conversation and he was smiling broadly. "More cavalry to the rescue, Ms. Judge?"

"Don't you have a home?" I asked.

He handed me a stainless steel bowl with all the shrimp offal. "You'd better get rid of this before it starts to smell."

I took the bowl without arguing, but only because I had ulterior motives. "Don't wait up," I said and stepped out on the porch in time to see Mickey Mantle go sailing by in his pickup, headed for the road.

Luckily, all I have to do is judge 'em; I don't have to catch 'em.

⌘

Mahlon and Guthrie were out working on the trawler as I dumped the shrimp heads and shells for the minnows and crabs to feed on. Back into the water from whence they came, I told myself. Ashes to ashes, sea to the sea.

Guthrie called a greeting and I didn't need a second invitation to walk over and see what they were up to.

They had almost finished getting all the juniper strips on the hull and the bow was an elegant flare that would soon be sanded smooth to receive its first coat of paint. The cabin was nearly ready for fitting out, but tonight their attention seemed centered on a large greasy piece of machinery that sat beside the boat on concrete blocks.

"Hey, you got your engine!" I said. "Andy's boys?"

"Yeah," Mahlon grunted as he secured a heavy chain around the thing.

"Drew and Maxton brought it just a little while ago," said Guthrie, with a face-splitting grin. "They were there when Andy first promised Grandpap, and they said they wouldn't go back on his word."

A trestle had been rigged over the open hole in the deck and now they were waiting for Mickey Mantle, who'd gone off somewhere to borrow a block and tackle so they could hoist the engine into place tonight.

In all the years that I'd been coming down, I'd never seen Mahlon work this steadily in one sustained effort. It was almost as if he believed that getting this boat completed and into the water would somehow put things back the way they were before so many rules and regulations began to endanger the different freedoms that gave meaning and substance to his life.

I could have told Kidd that the reason he hadn't caught Mahlon shooting at loons was because he was too busy shooting for something more important: his last chance at shaping a destiny for himself and Mickey Mantle and Guthrie, a chance for the two adults to get out from under, a chance for one more generation to live independent and unfettered.

The only fly in Guthrie's ointment that evening was worrying about how they were going to shift the boat off Linville Pope's property before she served them with papers for trespassing.

"We'll do it 'fore that time comes," Mahlon said gruffly as he picked up his hammer and fitted another strip of cypress to the hull.

"Didn't you hear?" I said. "She was killed this afternoon."

Even Mahlon quit work for that. They listened intently as I described what had happened; and as with Barbara Jean, Guthrie's first reaction was purely personal. "That mean them garbage men won't be back tomorrow?" he asked.

"Probably," I said.

"Good! Right, Grandpap? Now we don't have to shift her till she's done, do we?"

"Hand me them nails," Mahlon grunted. "You keep talking and not working and we'll never get her finished."

"Yonder comes Daddy," Guthrie said.

The truck headlights jounced down the rutted drive and Mickey Mantle made a skidding three-point turn so that the back of his truck was in position.

"Hey-o there, Judge!"

"I thought you had your license pulled," I said.

He grinned. "Judges don't write tickets, do they?"

"Daddy!" Guthrie interrupted. "Did you hear?" His changing voice squeaked in his excitement. He clambered up into the truck bed and handed out the block and tackle, chattering the whole time to his father about Linville's murder.

"Yeah, I just heard it. Sammy said it was on the news."

"Y'all here to talk or get this motor in?" said Mahlon. When they had the block and tackle attached to the trestle and a heavy cable fixed to the chain around the engine, they hooked the other end to the pickup. I volunteered to crank up the truck and pull the cable slow and steady for them while the three of them guided the heavy engine up over the side of the boat. Then I backed up so they could lower it into the hold.

"Damned if I don't feel like busting a bottle of beer over that engine right now!" Mickey Mantle said when the chains and cable were removed and the engine sat squarely where it was supposed to.

"Time enough for beers when we bring in our first catch," Mahlon said sharply. "Hand me my saw and let's get these last strips on 'fore midnight."

"Before I go," I said, "I need to ask you. Any of y'all see somebody break in over there this afternoon?"

That got their attention.

"Naw," said Mickey Mantle.

"I was fishing," said Mahlon.

"What'd they take?" asked Guthrie.

"Nothing, so far's I can tell," I admitted. "But they messed up Carl's lock and strewed my things around."

"I worn't here," Mahlon said again and revved up his Skilsaw with a conversation-stopping roar.

I waved goodnight and started back to the cottage, but as I circled the boat shed, I heard my name called in a voice so low that the noisy saw almost drowned it out.

It was Mahlon's wife. White-haired and half-crippled with arthritis, the reclusive Effrida beckoned to me from a darkened side window.

"I heared what you asked them," she said in an urgent rush of island speech. "I seen him, the man what broke into Carl's this evening. It was a few minutes after five."

"Did you know him?"

"I seen him before. Lives over to Beaufort, I think, but I couldn't call his name."

She then proceeded to describe Chet Winberry right down to the white fishing cap and navy-blue windbreaker he'd been wearing when Barbara Jean and I met him at their landing.

No wonder he'd caught only three fish all afternoon.

CHAPTER 12

There is a land of pure delight,
Where saints immortal reign;
There everlasting spring abides,
And never-withering flowers . . .
But tim'rous mortals start and shrink
To cross this narrow sea,
And linger, trembling on the brink,
And fear to launch away.

. . . Could we but climb where Moses stood,
And view the landscape o'er,
Not Jordan's stream nor death's cold flood
Should fright us from the shore.

—Isaac Watts

"A navy-blue windbreaker with attached hood," I raged to Kidd Chapin. "Remember how you thought last night's prowler was wearing a hooded jacket? The lying bastard! Pulled a muscle jogging for his newspaper this morning, did he? Too bad he didn't break his goddamned leg last night."

"Now hold on," said Kidd. "Just because he broke into your place doesn't mean he was the one you chased. Think about it. Why would he look for the papers over there if he thought they were here?"

"Because he didn't know they were here till this morning. Jay Hadley discussed it with Alliance members at Andy's funeral, but Chet was talking to someone else when they went into their huddle. Barbara Jean told him at breakfast that I had Andy's papers, and I bet he worked the conversation around to find out naturally so she doesn't suspect a thing. He must have searched the trunk of my car at noon and when he didn't find them there, he rode his boat over here."

I was furious when I thought of Chet's nice helpful offer to look over the papers for me because, quote, "I know most of the players."

Didn't he just, the bastard?

"Well at least he saved me some time," I told Kidd. "I was going to start with Linville's latest deals and then work back to the earliest. Now I'll start with the Ritchie House transaction."

While I retrieved the relevant documents from their hiding place between the newspaper sections and started laying them out in chronological order on the kitchen table, Kidd puttered quietly between refrigerator and sink and fixed me a shrimp salad.

It was delicious. "I didn't know I'd brought lettuce," I said.

"You didn't," he answered. "You also didn't bring the green peppers or the tomatoes. Or the pint of ice cream in the freezer."

"Ice cream?"

"Fudge Ripple." He cocked his long homely face at my interest. "If you're nice to me, I may let you have a spoonful."

"I'll take that under advisement," I said, feeling oddly comforted.

⌘

An hour later, I knew why Chet had tried so desperately to steal those papers.

It wasn't hard to find once I knew what I was looking for, although I still might have missed the significance if Andy hadn't practically drawn an arrow.

Twelve years ago, Linville Pope had bought from Ritchie Janson the waterfront property that later became the Ritchie House. She had put up her husband's dilapidated Morehead motel as part of the security. The rest was secured by the title to the *Washington Neville,* put up by Chester Amos Winberry with his power of attorney for Neville Fishery when he co-signed for the balance of the loan. The bank officer who approved the loan was probably one of Chet's good ol' buddies.

All done with a wink and a nod, no doubt.

"What's illegal about that?" asked Kidd.

"The thing is, he had a fiduciary interest in the property because he was also Ritchie Janson's attorney. Even if he were scrupulous about the actual sale—which, in point of fact, he wasn't—that would certainly get a jaundiced look from the Bar Association if it came out, although he does seem to have made Linville pay a fair price."

"How was he unscrupulous about the sale?"

"Look at the date Ritchie Janson's supposed to have signed the bill of sale."

"December fifth. And?"

"Now read his obituary notices from the local newspaper."

"Died December twenty-second after a lengthy hospital stay. Oh, so he let her take advantage of a really sick old man?"

"Not just sick, Kidd. Look at this letter to the editor where somebody wrote an appreciation of his life. See where she says that he lingered a month after his last stroke, but never regained consciousness? Not too many unconscious men sign bills of sale that I know of."

Kidd gave a low whistle. "Judge Winberry forged his signature?"

"He wasn't a judge back then." I leaned back in my chair, fitting all the pieces together. "What really must be tying a knot in his tail is that he used Barbara Jean's boat to start Linville Pope on a fast track that eventually threatened the things Barbara Jean values most."

"He must have been sleeping with her," said Kidd.

"Yes," I agreed slowly. "But he's so crazy about Barbara Jean."

"Not always a contradiction," he reminded me wryly.

"You know what this means, don't you?"

"What?"

"Except for Mahlon Davis—and he thinks everybody's out to get him, so it doesn't count—people say Andy was one of the most law-abiding men on the island. He wouldn't touch anybody's clam beds, they say, or take a scallop or oyster out of season, but he might bend the rules to protect members of the Alliance. Quig Smith says Andy made a phone call Sunday morning from Cab's and was looking at his watch like he had an appointment. What if he threatened to tell Barbara Jean what he'd found if Chet didn't get Linville to quit lobbying against commercial fishing? And what if he set up a meeting out on the water to hear Chet's answer?"

"And ol' Chet just happened to bring along a .22? Quig told me all his long guns were stolen."

"So he *says*. Very convenient theft, a day or two before Andy gets shot. And something else, Kidd—he was out on the water today when Linville was killed. If these documents were destroyed, who else would know or care enough to go back through all the public records and reassemble the proof that he was involved with her twelve years ago?"

"That's an awful big assumption you're making there, Ms. Judge. Maybe Bynum kept checking his watch so he'd know when the tide was low enough to dig clams."

I pushed away from the papers, overwhelmed with something close to nausea. I liked Chet and Barbara Jean. But I'd liked Andy and Linville, too, and it sickened me to think that one friend could kill another.

For a moment I felt like taking the advice given to Odysseus: I should put an oar on my shoulder and march inland until I got so far from the ocean and fishing and all these self-absorbed coastal conflicts that people would ask me what strange object I carried on my shoulder.

As if from far, far away, I heard Kidd's voice. "Ms. Judge?"

Abruptly, I stood and looked straight up into his hazel eyes. Our lips were only inches apart. "My name is Deborah."

"I knew that," he said, and bent to kiss me.

The kiss went on and on until it seemed we both must drown in Homer's wine-dark sea. Our lips parted for a moment and his breathing was as ragged as mine before he drew me to him again. Automatically, I started toward the bedroom, then hesitated. We weren't stupid teenagers any longer.

"I'm sorry," I whispered, "but we can't. I don't have any protect—"

He laid his fingers on my lips and gave a lopsided smile. "Now I don't want you to take this the wrong way, but lettuce and peppers and tomatoes and ice cream weren't all I brought with me this evening."

Delighted laughter suffused me. "I bet you were an Eagle Scout."

"*And* a member of the Optimists," he said solemnly.

⌘

It is absolutely true what they say about men with long thin fingers, but his hands were so gentle and so slow that I was roused to a frenzy before I finally found out for sure.

Afterward, when we lay tumbled and satisfied against the pillows and against each other, his hands lazily wandered across my body. "Anybody ever tell you what beautiful breasts you have?"

I gazed down at them in the semi-darkness of the room. "Eight-cow breasts," I said smugly.

"Huh?"

"There's this huge stack of *National Geographics* in our attic. When I started to develop, I got really self-conscious about it because all my friends were getting these little round scoops of ice cream and I was getting cones. Then I came across one of those pseudo-sociological studies of some African tribe—you know the kind of thing they used to do where they'd show the native women half naked, but the men were only photographed from the navel up so that you never got to see their manhood?"

He laughed. "Yeah, I remember."

"Well, according to the article, round-breasted women averaged six cows in the marriage market, but the fathers of cone-breasted women could get eight cows."

He cupped both of my breasts in his hands and kissed them. "These are worth at least ten."

"Are you saying I'm fat?" I asked, letting my own hands begin to wander.

"Not fat. But I do like knowing it's a woman in bed with me, okay?"

"Okay."

⌘

The nicest thing about the cottage's bathroom was that Carl had salvaged from somewhere an old claw-footed tub that was deep and wide and long enough for two. We ran it full of hot water, dumped in some bubble bath Celeste or Carlette must have left here once, and soaked for an hour, talking lazily about this and that. I knew that I'd have to go to Quig Smith tomorrow with what I'd found, but for tonight . . .

The telephone beside the bed rang sharply at eleven-ten.

"Deborah?" said my Aunt Zell. "Was that you I saw just now on the news, leaving the house where that Beaufort woman was murdered?"

I admitted it was and made light of my involvement. Aunt Zell doesn't fuss, but she does worry and she wasn't happy to think I'd stumbled into a second shooting.

"You take care of yourself, you hear?"

"I will," I promised, then told her goodnight and reached for Kidd.

I usually try to take Aunt Zell's advice whenever I can.

Besides, he was much, much better than Fudge Ripple ice cream.

CHAPTER 13

Throw out the Life-Line to danger-fraught men,
Sinking in anguish where you've never been:
Winds of temptation and billows of woe
Will soon hurl them out where the dark waters flow.

Throw out the Life-Line! Throw out the Life-Line!
Someone is drifting away;
Throw out the Life-Line! Throw out the Life-Line!
Someone is sinking today.

—Edward S. Ufford

Every morning, by the time I got vertical, Kidd Chapin had been gone, so when Mickey Mantle's banty roosters woke me at seven-thirty Friday morning, I was amused to turn over in bed and find his head still on the pillow beside me. Along with the rooster crows, a cool breeze drifted in through the open windows.

"No coffee in bed?" I asked, snuggling down under the quilt.

"Don't mind if I do," he yawned. "I'll take mine black."

I hit him with my pillow. "Just because you were top oyster last night doesn't mean I'm going to turn into Henrietta Hausfrau."

He let out a muffled yelp and wrapped those long skinny legs around mine.

"On the other hand," I said, wriggling free, "fair is fair, I suppose."

"And even in the morning, you're more than fair." He caught my hand and pulled me down for a long kiss that started at my lips and wound up on my breasts. "In fact," he said huskily, "I'll up my offer to twelve cows and a bushel of clams."

"Throw in a peck of oysters and I'll put in a good word for you with my daddy."

"Oysters are out of season," he murmured and began to do such entrancing things with my body that it was another twenty minutes before I got out of bed and said "Coffee" with much more firmness than I felt.

Jeans, sneakers and a Carolina sweatshirt, then out to the kitchen where I filled the coffee maker with cold water and measured out four scoops of a Kenyan blend I'd found in the freezer.

Andy Bynum's papers were on the table right where I'd left them last night and the sight of them rolled such a heavy black stone over my lighthearted mood that I grabbed up a bag of stale bread and told Kidd, "Let's go feed the gulls while the coffee's making."

"You do remember I'm supposed to be staking out loon hunters, don't you?"

"Mahlon won't know you're Wildlife. He'll just think I'm a loose woman."

He laughed. "You go ahead, I'll shave and start breakfast."

As I started out the door Kidd said, "Listen, Ms. Judge. You know what I said about oyster season? It really did close the thirty-first of March."

"So?"

"So maybe we ought to talk about it when you get back. Scrambled eggs or over easy for you?"

"Over easy," I said and went out into the bright April sunshine. The seriousness of his tone brought back that sinking feeling. Was this his tactful way of telling me that it'd been fun, but now the season was closed on any further relationship?

(*"One of these days you're going to remember that it's* caveat emptor," said the preacher.)

(*"Nothing wrong with* carpe diem," comforted the pragmatist.)

I was already into a Scarlett O'Hara mode on Chet, so I added Kidd to the things I'd think about later and surrendered myself to the delight of feeding gulls on the wing.

One or two are always cruising the shoreline and as soon as the first gull swooped to catch a bread morsel, a dozen more appeared from nowhere until the bright blue air around me was filled with flashing white wings. Playing the wind, they hovered over the water like hummingbirds in midair as I tossed the broken pieces high above me, then they wheeled and dipped and soared again until all my bread was gone.

As I turned back to land, Mahlon Davis greeted me from his porch with a smile that turned to a scowl when two large white trucks pulled into the lot beside his.

They were from that Morehead waste removal service that Linville Pope had hired to clear Mahlon's debris from her property. One had side railings for hauling, the other held a pint-size yellow bulldozer.

Mahlon's thin shoulders stiffened angrily as three muscular workmen got out of the trucks and began letting down a steel ramp to off-load the dozer.

"They must not know Linville Pope's dead," I said. Mahlon gave a threatening growl and struck off across the lot. I followed, sensing the beginning of a brawl. And wasn't I a judge? Didn't I know how to arbitrate?

By the time I picked my way through the junk and brambles, things had already begun to escalate. Mahlon's accent was too thick to let me distinguish his stream of angry threats, but evidently the workmen were understanding every abusive term. One of them had grabbed a shovel from the back of the truck and looked as if it wouldn't take much more before he swung it at Mahlon's head.

As I approached, Mahlon said to me, "Them bastards're saying if I don't move my boat they're going to push it off."

"We got our orders from the property owner," said the beefiest of the three men. He had a clipboard in his hand and he thumped the flimsy yellow top sheet.

"From Linville Pope?"

"That's right, lady."

"But she was killed yesterday," I said.

"See?" said Mahlon. "And she's a judge. She knows the law."

"You really a judge?" asked the man.

I nodded.

"And Mrs. Pope really *is* dead?"

"Yes."

The man with the shovel lowered it and the other workman loosened his clenched fists. It looked for a moment as if that might be that, but their boss stood firm and said, "Well, ma'am, I'm real sorry to hear she's dead and all, but she put a deposit down and we signed a contract and far as I'm concerned, that's something him and the lawyers can work out. I need this job and I'm going to do it less'n you want to serve me with papers to quit."

He had me there and he knew it. He looked at Mahlon. "We'll start on the other side, but when we get to this side, mister, if you ain't moved that boat, I promise you we're going to move it for you." Again he thumped his clipboard. "She made a particular point of that boat in this contract."

"The hell you say!" howled Mahlon. As he stormed across the lot back to his shed, he was cursing so loud and so viciously that I was glad Guthrie was at school and not around to hear or get cuffed in his anger.

"Now listen," I said to the boss. "Can't you—"

"Uh-oh!" said the youngest workman and he quickly headed for the near truck, just as a shot rang out.

I whirled and there stood Mahlon at the front of his boat shed with a rifle in his hands and I could only watch in stunned horror as he fired again. As if in slow motion, I heard it hit the truck behind us. Another sharp crack and the boss worker crumpled beside me. Blood splattered across the yellow contract on his clipboard and jerked me back to real time.

"Mahlon, my God! What are you doing?" I screamed and ran toward him. "Stop!"

He banged off another shot at the other two men who were diving for cover, but as I got to him, he suddenly swung the .22 to point straight at me. Such hot rage blazed in his eyes that it hit me I was looking down the barrel at Andy and Linville's killer.

Oysters, I thought inanely. That's what Kidd meant. A week into April, on a tide-washed sandbar where oysters don't grow, yet I'd seen a half-dozen scattered there near the body of a man who would never take a shellfish out of season. And that night Guthrie had come across in the twilight to say "Grandpap brought home some oysters today and Granny says do you want some?"

"Don't do this, Mahlon," I pleaded, but even as I spoke, the barrel swung to the right and he fired toward the road. Almost deafened by the explosion, I looked back in time to see Kidd duck down behind a Carteret County patrol car that had pulled up beside the cottage. The shot spiderwebbed its windshield.

Then I felt the hot barrel between my shoulder blades and Mahlon yelled, "Y'all keep away from me! Y'all don't get back, I'll shoot her. I swear to God I will."

I saw Kidd straighten up and I screamed, "Stay back!" Then Mahlon prodded me. "Walk on the other side of the boat," he ordered.

Numbly, I went. Around on the seaward side, blocks and boxes formed rough steps that led up to the boat railing for easy access over the side. Prodded by the rifle barrel, I went up and over and Mahlon followed till we reached the unfinished cabin and looked out through glassless window holes.

We were six feet or more above the ground, almost parallel to the shoreline. To the left was the sea. To the right, houses and the road beyond. The man Mahlon had shot lay motionless in the weed-filled lot. Cars were stopping along the road edge beyond Clarence Willis's trailer, and knots of people stared and pointed to us. I couldn't see Kidd, but someone was crouched behind the patrol car and I heard the crackle of a two-way radio, so professional help was probably on the way if someone didn't do something stupid first.

"Mahlon, listen to me," I said. "It doesn't have to be like this."

"Shut up!" he snarled. Then almost immediately, "All I ever did was mind my own business and try to make a living and they won't let me."

"But Andy lent you money," I said softly. "He gave you an engine."

"No, he didn't!"

"But—"

"I seen him Saturday night and maybe I might've had a beer or two too many, but he talked to me like I was dirt. Said I was too sorry to finish a boat. Said if I did, I'd probably wreck it like the other one. Said his mind was full changed and he won't gonna throw good money after bad. Next day I'd been out and shot me a turtle and was coming in with some oysters, too, when I seen him over yonder clamming and I went out to talk to him reasonable-like to see if he'd change his mind back 'cause I had to have that motor and *he* certainly worn't using it. I even tried to give him some of my oysters and he started yelling about taking stuff out of season, when hell, season hadn't even been closed a week. Besides, I didn't get 'em to sell, they was for us to eat. And he said men like me was what was holding back his shitty Alliance. Said he'd see me in hell 'fore I'd get so much as a net sinker out of him so I grabbed out my gun and said well say hello to the devil for me."

Carefully, I turned till I was facing him and the gun was only inches from my chest. "Mahlon, what you did was in the heat of the moment. I'm not saying you'll get off scot-free, but it's not half as bad as if you stand up here and think about it and then shoot somebody else."

His unshaven chin clenched tightly and his glittering eyes darted wildly from my face to the men who'd gathered behind the patrol car.

"All I wanted was to be left alone so me and my boys could make a living like we always done. But they keep changing it, telling us we can't do this, we can't do that, and Andy worn't gonna let me have the engine and that bitch over to Beaufort worn't gonna let me finish building the boat. I told her just give me till the end of May and me and my boys'll pick up every scrap of our stuff. It worn't doing her no harm, but she just stood there on the end of her landing like she owned the world and everything in it and said she'd given me all the time I was going to get from her."

"She shouldn't have said that," I soothed, "but think of Guthrie, Mahlon. How's he going to feel if he comes home from school and hears you've killed innocent people that never did you any harm?"

"Turn around," he said.

"Mahlon—"

He jammed the rifle barrel into my stomach. "Dammit, I said turn around!"

I turned and a dozen thoughts crowded through my head at once: how sad my daddy was going to be and my brothers, but at least it'd be quick and— "Kidd, no! Go back!"

Again that deafening explosion of the gun in my ear and an instant of bewilderment until the rifle crashed to the deck behind me.

When I looked back, Mahlon had slumped against the cabin ledge, a bloody hole beneath his chin.

CHAPTER 14

O sinners, the heralds of mercy implore,
They cry like the patriarch, "Come."
The Ark of salvation is moored to your shore,
Oh, enter while yet there is room!
The stormcloud of Justice rolls dark overhead,
and when by its fury you're tossed,
Alas, of your perishing souls 'twill be said,
"They heard—they refused—and were lost!"

—Kate Harrington

"You suspected Mahlon Davis all the time?" I asked.

"Well, him and three more," said Quig Smith. "One of the neighbors saw him coming in from that direction around one o'clock."

We were seated at the kitchen table sharing a six-pack and a big bag of corn chips. It was a little before twelve and the rescue wagon had been and gone twice; the first time with the seriously wounded waste disposal man, the second time with Mahlon's body. Except for a steady stream of island neighbors bringing food and comfort to Mahlon's family, the crowds had dispersed and there was little to show for what had taken place that morning.

At last things had quieted down enough for Quig to take our statements and to satisfy my unanswered questions.

I rooted around in the refrigerator and found pimento cheese and some stuffed olives, which I set on the table. "Who were the others?"

"Remember how Jay Hadley tried to make us think the whole family went to church Sunday morning?"

"Yeah?"

"Her son Josh was seen out near the lighthouse around eleven and then again at one. He's sixteen and a hothead and we heard he didn't like Andy flirting with his mom. Then there was Scratch Kinlow. You know him?"

I shook my head.

"Lives on the north side of the island. He tried to punch Andy out over the weight of his catch last month, and he made some serious threats. Nobody actually saw him out near Shackleford, but his buddy was there and you don't usually see the one without the other."

"What about Chet Winberry?"

"The judge?" He rubbed his chin and gave me a quizzical look. "You thought maybe him?"

"Well you were the one asking me at Andy's funeral how good a friend he was, and it *was* awfully convenient that his guns got stolen when they did."

"Oh, they turned up yesterday evening. Pawnshop over in Havelock."

I was too embarrassed to tell him my theories. That first day in his office, he'd reminded me that some men took messing with their livelihoods more serious than somebody messing with their wives, but had I listened? No, I'd gone looking for fancy upstate motives instead of basic bedrock.

And Kidd sat there through the whole exchange, eating corn chips and pimiento cheese with a bland expression on his face, and never said a word about fiduciary trusts, the Ritchie House or forged signatures. Who can find a virtuous man who doesn't blab everything he knows? His price is above rubies.

"Sure would have helped if you'd thought to mention about Davis bringing in oysters last Sunday," Quig said as he popped a final olive in his mouth and rose to go.

"If you'd told *me* about oysters being out of season and not growing on tidal sandbars," I reminded him, "maybe I would've."

"We gotta get her a schedule and teach her some rudiments of marine biology," Quig told Kidd. "And that reminds me. You gonna be at the clean water hearing tonight?"

"No, I don't think so," said Kidd.

Quig grinned. "Naw, I didn't think you would."

While Kidd walked out to the car with him, I called Chet's number.

"Deborah!" he said. "You just missed Barbara Jean. She's gone anti-quing with a friend over near Goldsboro."

Was his tone a little too hearty?

"That's good," I said evenly, "because it's you I'm coming to see."

⌘

Kidd rode over with me.

The light on the Earl C. Davis Memorial Bridge went from green to yellow and I accelerated across before it could draw up to let a tall-masted boat through.

"Who was Earl C. Davis anyhow?" I wondered aloud when I was safely on the other side.

"Owen and Earl/Own the world./Watch out! Soon/They'll own the moon."

"Huh?"

"That's what they used to say down here when I was a little boy. Right after the moon landing. I guess Owen Fulcher and Earl Davis were supposed to be sharp traders."

"Like Linville Pope?"

"Don't know, Ms. Judge."

We rode in silent thought through Bettie, then across North River, and south on Highway 70. When we neared the outskirts of Beaufort, Kidd said, "What are you going to do with those papers?"

"What should I do with them?"

"Not for me to say."

⌘

I left Andy's papers locked in the trunk.

Chet seemed not to have heard of the morning's events and I was too edgy to tell him. He was surprised to see Kidd with me, but made a smooth recovery as he showed us out to the sunlit terrace and said, "Get anybody a drink?"

I refused and Kidd allowed as how maybe he'd walk down to Chet's landing. "Give y'all a chance to talk."

"He knows, doesn't he?" Chet asked, sitting heavily in one of the Adirondack chairs beneath the purple wisteria.

"Yes, but no one will ever hear it from him."

"What about you?"

"Chet—"

"Look, I'm not going to beg. Just try to understand, okay! Between Jill starting to date and the fishery, too, Barbara Jean had her hands so full that she didn't have any time left over for me."

"And Linville did?"

"She was the one who encouraged me to get into politics. My career was going nowhere till then. I was just a small-town attorney, tending to the legal needs of my father-in-law's business. Hell, Deborah, half my outside clients were court-appointed."

He got up and freshened his drink. "Sure I can't—?"

"No."

"You don't make it easy, girl."

"News flash, Chet: not every 'girl' is in your world to smooth things over for you."

He sighed. "I don't see what the big deal is. Nobody got hurt. The Janson estate got every penny it had coming. If I hadn't let Mr. Janson sell it to Linville—"

I arched my eyebrows. "*Let* him sell? A man in a coma?"

"Then you do know everything," he said, with a sick look on his face.

"I think so. Yes."

"All the same," he argued, "the old inn was falling down. It couldn't stand to wait another year while the heirs finished bickering. By that time, the roof would have fallen in and they'd have gotten a lot less than Linville paid."

"A preservationist *and* a humanitarian," I gibed.

Chet flushed. "You think I haven't kicked myself a hundred times since then? Especially when Linville started after Neville Fishery. She'd never put the screws to me. That wasn't her style. But just knowing that I was the one who gave her the start that she built on has been pure hell these last six months."

"I can believe that," I said.

Encouraged, he leaned forward. "What I did was wrong. I admit it. But don't think it hasn't eaten at me all these years. I know people say I go too easy on white-collar defendants sometimes, but whenever some poor slob comes up before me embezzling a few thousand, or cheating on his taxes, I have to think that there but for the grace of God. Everybody's done things they're ashamed of, Deborah. Haven't you?"

"Of course."

"Not that it's an excuse. But when you know how much some people are getting away with and what you've done hasn't really hurt anybody—" He sighed, set his drink on the wide arm of his chair, stretched his long legs straight out till he was nearly horizontal, and in a tone so low I almost couldn't hear, he muttered, "Shared shabbiness."

"What?"

"That's what I call it. When we tell ourselves everybody's doing it and most are doing worse. The small shabby things we do that make us not point the finger at someone else. A shared complicity. But every time we do it, a little more decency leaks away from us, a little more glory gone from our world. Take Andy Bynum. He actually apologized to me, but he said he couldn't figure any other way to get Linville to keep her mouth shut about commercial fishing in close. Said blackmailing me like that wasn't half as bad as signing Ritchie Janson's signature."

I stood and as if I'd jerked a string, Kidd started up from the landing.

"What are you going to do?" Chet asked.

(*"You don't bring down a fellow judge,"* the pragmatist reminded me. *"Not if you want to be known as a team player."*)

(*"Right is right,"* said the preacher inexorably.)

Shared shabbiness or holier than thou? I didn't like either choice.

He read the decision in my eyes and leaned back in his chair with his own eyes closed.

"I'm sorry, Chet," I told him.

And I was.

⌘

"Why don't you head straight on down Front Street?" said Kidd. "I'll buy you a beer at the Dock House and we'll look at all the rich people in their boats and I'll tell you about the time I found a fish trap at a creek off Kerr Lake."

"Okay." I didn't trust my voice to say more.

"Hey, you're not crying because you're going to unseat that sorry bastard, are you?"

"No." We both knew I was lying.

"Okay," he said. "So what happened was I had to sit on that fish trap for three solid days before anybody came to check on it."

He spotted the tissue holder over the sun visor on his side and handed me a couple without breaking his narration. It was very long and very complicated. Something to do with a six-five, three-hundred-pound gorilla of a man who brought along three little younguns when he came to empty his illegal fish trap. The story lasted all the way till we were seated at a small table on an upstairs porch overlooking the marina, and by that time I was resigned to doing the right thing and was ready to, if not laugh, at least relax.

To my bemusement, I spotted Lev on the deck of the *Rainmaker* with Catherine Llewellyn's young son in his arms. Claire Montgomery's hand puppet seemed to be entertaining them both as the Llewellyns themselves arrived with a couple of large suitcases. I realized they must be getting ready to leave.

Poor Lev, I thought, picturing the rest of a life co-opted by Catherine Llewellyn. No doubt she'll allow him one-night stands, but I also have no doubt that she'll make very, very sure (ever so solicitously, and for his own good, of course) that he never again gets entangled by someone who could disengage him from her orbit.

Already Lev was taking on the outlines of a Proust novel—something I know that I read and absorbed, yet can no longer remember why, nor even if, I actually enjoyed it.

"See somebody you recognize?" Kidd asked.

"No," I said. "No, I don't."

CHAPTER 15

My life flows on in endless song;
Above earth's lamentation,
I hear the sweet tho' far-off hymn
That hails a new creation;
Thro' all the tumult and the strife
I hear the music ringing;
It finds an echo in my soul—
How can I keep from singing?

—Anonymous

"All things considered," said F. Roger Longmire when he finally got through to me next morning, "I'm gonna tell Judge Mercer's chief to find someone else to sub for Mercer next week. Harrison Hobart can still sit in for you in Dobbs if you want to take a couple of days off."

"That's okay," I told him. "I'll be fine by Monday, but thanks, Roger."

While we'd talked, Kidd had cleaned the bathroom and swabbed down the kitchen floor. There was nothing else to do except finish packing and run the vacuum over the carpet in the rest of the cottage. Sue keeps the place like a dollhouse and no way was I going to leave it less than pristine.

Kidd was so anxious for us to get going that he'd already brought in the rocking chair from the porch and had to lift it up while I vacuumed underneath.

"Won't have to be this fussy at *my* place," he said as I stashed the vacuum in the closet.

I doubted that. Last night, when he was talking me into finishing the weekend at his cabin on the banks of the Neuse near New Bern, he'd described it with such pride of ownership that it wouldn't be too many notches below Sue's standards.

"Long as you have clean sheets," I said.

We loaded the cars—we'd retrieved his from Shell Point last night and would caravan back to New Bern—and I walked out to turn off the water and lock up the pump house.

I glanced over toward Mahlon's house where all was silent. Mickey Mantle had gone roaring out alone on his truck an hour or so ago. I couldn't tell if Effrida was inside there or not, but I spotted Guthrie sitting at the very end of the ramshackle pier gazing over the water to Shackleford Banks and I walked down to join him.

He didn't look around though he must have felt my footsteps along the rickety planks.

"I didn't want to leave without saying goodbye," I said.

The empty skiff was tied up to the piling beside him and it bobbed up and down in the gentle waves. I guess it really was his now.

"I never did get you a real mess of clams," Guthrie said.

"Next time," I said. "Guthrie, I'm really sorry—"

"Me and Daddy, we're going to finish the boat and fish her like Grandpap wanted us to do." There was a fiercely dogged look on his face. The wind whipped his sun-bleached hair straight back and I saw that his eyes were red-rimmed and bloodshot. "Daddy says we'll take her up around Norfolk when she's finished. Maybe even hire us a couple of men and go fish off New Jersey. You'n catch more fish up there in one day than you can in a whole week down here 'cause the water's colder. We're gonna do real good."

I wanted to hug him like one of my nephews. Instead, I held out my hand and he shook it solemnly.

"Don't you worry," he said. "We're gonna do fine."

At the cottage, Kidd was waiting at the wheel of his car.

I turned the key in the new lock we'd installed, then got into my car and switched on the ignition.

At the end of the driveway, as I waited for Kidd to pull out onto the road, I glanced back in my rearview mirror. Sunlight sparkled on the water, blue sky gleamed through the empty windows of the unfinished trawler, and out on the landing, Guthrie sat motionless with his face to the sea.

About Margaret Maron

Margaret Maron is the author of thirty novels and two collections of short stories. Winner of several major American awards for mysteries (Edgar, Agatha, Anthony, Macavity), her works are on the reading lists of various courses in contemporary Southern literature and have been translated into 17 languages. She has served as president of Sisters in Crime, the American Crime Writers League, and Mystery Writers of America.

A native Tar Heel, she still lives on her family's century farm a few miles southeast of Raleigh, the setting for *Bootlegger's Daughter*, which is numbered among the 100 Favorite Mysteries of the Century as selected by the Independent Mystery Booksellers Association. In 2004, she received the Sir Walter Raleigh Award for best North Carolina novel of the year. In 2008, she was honored with the North Carolina Award for Literature. (The North Carolina Award is the state's highest civilian honor.) In 2013, Mystery Writers of America named her Grand Master, its highest award. In 2015, the World Mystery Convention awarded her with its Lifetime Achievement Award. In 2016, she was inducted into the North Carolina Literary Hall of Fame.